UGLY STORIES ABOUT TERRIBLE PEOPLE DOING HORRIBLE THINGS

VOLUME ONE

Advance reviews for
UGLY STORIES ABOUT TERRIBLE PEOPLE DOING HORRIBLE THINGS, VOL. ONE:

"Monstrous. Macabre. Marvelously disturbed. Any horror fan knows that maintaining an aura of the unexpected is vital for maximum enjoyment and thrills, and I'm pleased to say that Elliott managed to achieve just that." - Jordan Murray

"This book will have you liking characters that you would otherwise hate, cheering for victims of "horrible things", and enjoying stories that make you wonder if there is something wrong with you for loving it so much!" - Amanda Tonkin

"Elliott masterfully weaves nostalgia and horror into a tapestry of unforgettable stories, each followed by the author's personal notes that offer a tantalizing glimpse into the warped mind behind the woe." - Dr. Marie Lestrange, Author of *CRIMSON COBBLESTONES*

"Tobin uses real-life experiences in these stories, which is part of what makes them that much more creepy and harrowing." - Samantha Mannone

"These are not just stories. These are a trauma informed hellish landscape filled with real, imagined (and projected) monsters. Elliott has taken his life experiences, his demons and his curiosities and banished them into a book where we can all witness the blood sport." - Diane Klaver

"A theme within Tobin's writing…is his examination of the evil that men (and women) do. Even when it comes to his supernatural monsters, their evils always feel so mortal and real." - Jonny Ward

"An impressive collection of short fiction with a decidedly disturbing undercurrent." - Nicole Haugen

"Elliott masterfully weaves dark tales that will make even the most desensitized horror fan shiver." - TJ Hodder

"Tobin has filled this book with heart-tugging, gut-wrenching tales that pull you in and make you forget that they're fiction, even when they completely sidestep reality." - S. Elizabeth Ransdell

Other Books by Tobin Elliott

The Aphotic Series

Bad Blood
Out For Blood
Blood Loss
Blood Pact
Blood Relations
Flesh and Blood

Story Collections

Ugly Stories About Terrible People Doing Horrible Things, Vol. 1
Ugly Stories About Terrible People Doing Horrible Things, Vol. 2

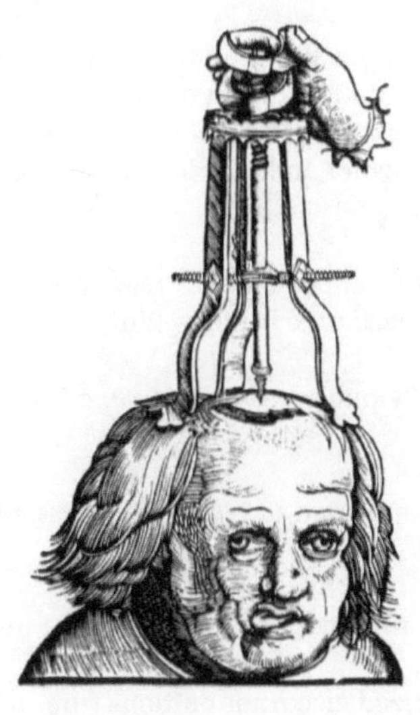

UGLY STORIES ABOUT TERRIBLE PEOPLE DOING HORRIBLE THINGS

VOLUME ONE

Tobin Elliott

Copyright @ 2024 Tobin Elliott

Luminous Aphotica Publishing

All rights reserved. No part of this publication may be reproduced, stored in a retrieval system, or transmitted in any form or by any process—electronic, mechanical, photocopying, recording, or otherwise—without the prior written permission of the copyright owner and Luminous Aphotica Publishing, except for brief quotations in a review.

"Scooter's Last Run" originally appeared as "Prison Break" in *Expiration Date,* published by EDGE Science Fiction & Fantasy, 2015

"The Wrong Child" originally published as *Vanishing Hope,* by Burning Effigy Press, 2011

"Stealing Corey" originally appeared in *Whispered Words,* published by Piquant Press, 2012

"Done" originally appeared in *Blood Loss,* published by Luminous Aphotica, 2023

Please purchase only authorized electronic editions from reliable retailers. In doing so, you support the authors and respect their rights. Seriously kids, piracy is bad.

This is a work of fiction. All of the characters, organizations, and events portrayed in these stories are either the product of the authors' imagination or are used fictitiously.

ISBN 978-1-998827-09-1 (hardcover)
ISBN 978-1-998827-08-4 (paperback)
ISBN 978-1-998827-10-7 (ebook)

Cover Design by Camille Codling
(Instagram: @codling.creations)

This one is for, as always, my family who puts up with all this weird shit I write.

It's for Ms. Roberts, my grade eight English teacher who encouraged me more than she ever knew.

It's for the creative writing teacher who praised the silly little scene I wrote that ended up sparking BLOOD LOSS.

But it's also for both the editors who read my stories and thought they were good enough to publish, as well as the editors who turned me down, for whatever reasons.

Special shout out to my ID Press compatriots, Connie Di Pietro, Pat Flewwelling, Dale Long, and A.L. Tompkins. You pushed me when I needed to be pushed.

In every case, I ended up with some cool stories to put in these collections.

I'd like to take a moment to acknowledge my early readers who provided me with invaluable advance reviews, feedback, and error detection.

Every one of you helped make this book better.

Nicole Haugen
TJ Hodder from Tapes of Trepidation
Diane Klaver
Dr. Marie Lestrange
Samantha Mannone
Jordan Murray
Liz Ransdell
Amanda Tonkin
Jonny Ward

If you spot mistakes, don't blame any of these people. That's all on me.

What ugly sights of death within mine eyes!

Shakespeare
Richard III

CONTENTS

WELCOME TO MY NIGHTMARES

[I THINK YOU'RE GONNA LIKE THEM]

"WHAT ARE YOU working on now?"

That's gotta be the bane of every author's existence, that question. And it always seems to be one of the final questions on every podcast or online interview that I've participated in.

I can't speak for other authors, because every one of us is different, and we all have our own ways of navigating this writing thing. I know authors that dutifully plug away at one thing at a time, setting it up and knocking it down. I know others that go in infrequent spurts of creativity, going months without even trying to write, then spitting out brilliance in the span of a few days, only to let the computer collect dust again for a few months. And, of course, everything in between.

For me however, "what are you working on now?" is a complicated question. Because my brain is a complicated thing like a pinball bouncing all over the place, sometimes trying to just stop, only to get paddled back into action again.

Stories come at me from everywhere, but rarely do they land fully formed. I'll hear or read or see something that'll light up one part of the pinball game of my mind. I'll think, *damn, that's cool. That should go in a story.* Like, for instance, someone telling me in the early 1980s that their lover yells, "Geronimo!" when they orgasm.

Sat on that one for damn near forty years, but I used it.

Sometimes it's a confluence of things piling up over a few days or weeks. A strange factoid about an author from two-hundred years ago, stacked on top of weird news story, stacked on top of Bee Gees lyrics.

My point is, at any one time, I may have little groups of these confluences all vying for my attention, waiting for that one last tweak to make the story come alive. So I'll have several files at various stages of completion patiently waiting for me.

The true, unvarnished answer to the question then is, "Well, I've got a novel that's about two-thirds finished, I'm also working on two others with a co-author, as well as a clean-up of one we've finished. I had that non-fiction book that I just finished last week. I have this idea for another novel that's percolating, and then there's all these little story bits that will become short stories. Other than that, not much."

Welcome to my hoarder's brain. No good idea goes unpunished.

FOR SOME REASON, I find novels easier to work out that a simple short story, maybe because I have room to sprawl out and get in all the fun little things I want to get in.

Shorter works are far more nitpicky.

A few of the stories you'll read in this collection, or its second volume companion, were written for submissions I'd heard about. But I do have the most annoying habit of going long.

So, this submission needs 2,000 words or less? Yeah, my story will be double that. That one will accept up to 5,000 words? Fantastic! Would you consider the one I wrote that ended up at 12,000 words?

No?

Damn.

Consider the first volume in this collection—and go ahead and think the same about volume two—as that scene in some nautical movie where they stumble upon the graveyard of ships. These are all the stories that couldn't make the limitations of submission calls, or they sat half-written for decades, or, in some rare cases, they actually did get published, and I still like them enough to collect them here.

This is my graveyard of ships stories that went around the world and drifted back to me.

It's my Island of Misfit Toys stories that nobody wanted.

It's my junk drawer of tales mostly unread.

But between this and volume two?

It's also some of my favourite writing.

I hope you enjoy reading these as much as I enjoyed frankensteining them together.

Tobin Elliott
July 2024

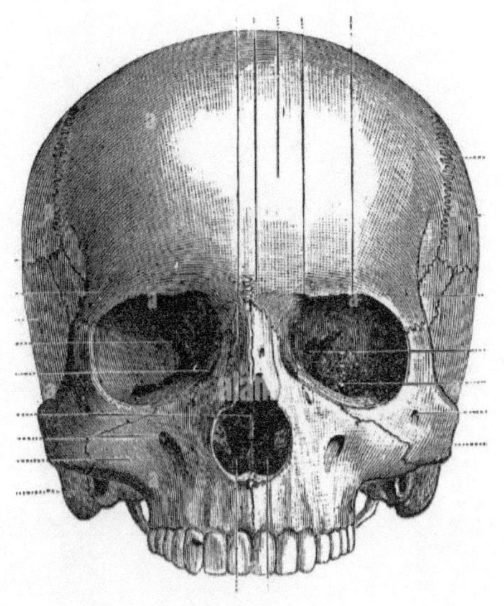

PART ONE:
FRIENDS & FAMILY

"The saddest thing about betrayal
is that it never comes from your enemies,
it comes from those you trust the most."

Unknown

SCOOTER'S LAST RUN

THE LAST TIME Scooter ran away, I was six years old.

My mom and dad had split up a year before and we'd had to move. My dad wouldn't take my dog, Scooter, and Mom and I couldn't have him in the apartment we moved to. The next best thing was to give him a good home so we arranged to have him live with George and Carol Black, friends of ours that lived not too far away. I hung out with their daughter, Debbi—and yes, there were the inevitable comments about how nice it would be if we grew up and got married that always got our eyes rolling. But at least I had a place to visit my dog. And make no mistake, no matter where Scooter lived, he was *my* dog.

We'd got him three years earlier, back when Mom and Dad still talked nicely to each other. Dad came home with a small, black, brown-eyed squirming bundle of joy and it was love at first sight for both of us. Though he was a black Lab, he had a small white patch over the toes of both hind legs that, in my mind, just made him even more fascinating. When my parents asked me what I wanted to name him, I picked Scooter. Don't ask why. The fog of time has eradicated whatever reason my three-year-old brain may have come up with.

Then my parents split up. We moved into an apartment, my father moved in with his sister, and Scooter went to our family friends, the Blacks. I don't think any one of us were happy with the new status quo, but the only one that actively protested it was Scooter. Every few months, he'd slip his collar and head home. Well, what he thought of as home.

And to be honest, it was still the place I considered home as well. The place with the backyard, the small pond, the wooded area that was safe for a six-year-old to roam in...all of it now replaced by a cramped apartment with a balcony and hallways that smelled of old fried food and damp laundry. There was a park across the street now, but I couldn't play hide and seek in a flat plain broken only with a battered swing set. I missed my magical woods.

I guess Scooter did too. The first time he left the Black's, they phoned in a panic, but it wasn't even an hour later we got the call that Scooter was sitting in his old dog house back at our old house, now owned by someone that I felt couldn't ever understand how great the place was. They didn't have a dog. They didn't even have kids.

When we went to get Scooter that first time, he seemed quite pleased with himself that he'd been able to draw everyone back home. His thick black tail thumped the wall of the dog house as we approached, gently admonishing him. Then his big brown eyes seemed to radiate disappointment when we bundled him into my mother's sky blue '62 Pontiac and took him back to George and Carol.

A few weeks later, he did it again. I'm sure in his little doggy brain he was hoping *this* time he would succeed in getting home.

It happened a third and fourth and fifth time. By then, it was a routine. We smilingly referred to them as Scooter's "prison breaks". George and Carol would first call us to alert us, then call the residents of the old house to keep an eye out. By the fifth time, we just drove over and waited for him to show. When he came bounding through the woods and trotted across the yard to me as I waited by his dog house, I could almost read it in his eyes, in the way he loped across the lawn, in the set of his mouth as his tongue bobbed out and looking for all the world like he was smiling. *Finally!* I'm sure he thought. *I finally got them trained!*

We took him back to George and Carol who, as usual, apologized profusely. I never minded. I got to spent time with my dog in the back seat of Mom's car. But handing him over to George and Carol... Man, it was like giving him up all over again. Every time.

I made sure that, each time I walked Scooter back to the Black's back yard and slipped the collar over his head and tightened it up, that I would stroke his shiny black head, look directly into his eyes and tell him how much I loved him and how, someday, we'd be able to live together again in a nice house with a nice yard and some woods to walk in. I didn't realize until the fourth or fifth time that I also had a grip on his dog tag, the one with his name on it, and I was rubbing it between my thumb and fingers.

THE LAST TIME he ran away, it started the same as every other prison break. We got the call from Carol. Mom and I hopped in the Pontiac and headed over to the old place and then we waited.

We'd never had to wait over an hour.

This time, we were there almost four hours before we gave up. I didn't like the lines in my mother's forehead or the set of her mouth.

We called the old place when we got back, sure that Scooter would have shown up just after we left. No, they hadn't seen him yet. They'd keep an eye out and call as soon as he showed.

The next day, I came home from school and, before I could say anything, I knew Mom hadn't heard anything. The lines in her forehead were etched a little deeper. The set of her mouth a little more engrained.

By the end of the week, my mom began laying down comments about Scooter maybe not coming back this time. That maybe this time he was gone. "Gone for good," was the line she used, though I could see nothing good about it.

That weekend, we stopped by George and Carol's place. By now, the apologetic refrain had been memorized, but they really stepped it up. I didn't say anything, because I knew if I did, I'd yell at how they didn't fix the stupid issue and allow him to escape a half-dozen times. But I also knew no one had taken it seriously, so the blame rested with all of us.

Instead, I walked to the back yard. I found his collar, still attached to the end of a length of plastic-covered wire clothesline. And hanging from the collar, Scooter's dog tag. Without really thinking about it, I unhooked the tag and, with a quick rub between my fingers and a whispered, "Please come back, Scooter," I pocketed it.

Over the next few weeks, the drudgery of day-to-day living, work for Mom, school and homework for me, crept back and did its best to pluck thoughts of my lost dog out of our minds. It mostly worked for my mother, who mentioned him less and less. But for me, I entered into a ritual that would ensure I would never forget my dog.

Each night, as I got into bed, I pulled out the dog tag from its hiding place under my bedside light and I would rub it between thumb and forefinger and whisper "Please come back, Scooter."

THREE MONTHS LATER, I was over at George and Carol's, having spent the afternoon playing with Debbi. It was now a warm, drowsy afternoon and we were both sprawled on the couch watching an old Tarzan movie. Debbi always had a thing for Johnny Weissmuller, so I guess watching him jump around in nothing but a loincloth worked for her.

My eyes were closing as I settled in for an afternoon nap when I heard a faint noise at their front door. I ignored it and shifted to get more comfortable. Then I heard it again. A scratching.

Like a dog scratching at the aluminum screen door.

"Scooter!" I yelled and ran for the door.

My dog lay at the front door, his sides heaving. He couldn't stand, but George, hearing my excitement, came running and picked him up and brought him inside. I noticed the streak of blood on the screen door from where Scooter had let us know he'd made it back.

His paws were bloody and his tongue lolled lifelessly, but he looked at me and his eyes spoke to me. "I came back to you. You believed I would and I did." George took off the new collar and the five feet or so of chain lead that Scooter had dragged with him from wherever he'd come from.

George examined him and said that, aside from his paws, he seemed fine, just exhausted. He was going to be all right.

Tears came quickly to my eyes and I thrust my hand into my pocket and clutched at the dog tag. Squeezing my hand and eyes tight, I whispered a thank you to whatever force brought my dog back to me.

♦ ♦ ♦

IT WAS THE last time he ever ran away.

THAT WAS BACK in 1968. Today, almost sixty years later, I watch Scooter as he pulls his old, old bones up and makes his way over to his food dishes to listlessly lap at the water. Most of his fur is gone now, and what's left is white. His flesh hangs off him like the skin of some rotted fruit. It's pulled down from his eyes, leaving those once-clear brown eyes recessed into sagging folds that constantly run with waxy fluids. I hear his bones clicking as he walks or moves in any way.

But by far, the worst of it is whenever he lowers his hindquarters in preparation to lie down. Every time he does it, Scooter's hips break. I hear them. I see his body jerk with the pain. But somehow, things go back to normal and, after a couple of hours or so, he's able to slowly get up again. Somehow the bones knit and the sockets are reslotted.

I know it has something to do with that dog tag.

It's something that I should have taken care of years ago. Decades ago.

I should have let go years ago.

But Scooter's been my dog now for almost six decades. I'd even managed to make good on my promise and I'd given him a nice house with a nice yard that backed on some woods. We'd walked those woods almost every day for years and years and years.

I should have let go years, ago, but it's hard to let go of the pet that taught you that miracles can happen.

He watches me as I take my coffee out to the back porch. I don't take him with me anymore as he can't make it down the three stairs to the deck, though his fleshless tail sways from side to side in a parody of its youthful exuberance. I give him a sad smile as I walk around the corner of the house and settle into the porch swing and sip my coffee.

I get myself ready. Mentally prepare myself. I've decided.

Today's the day.

I reach into my pocket and pull out the worn dog tag. I've rubbed it so much over the years that only the *S* and the *R* are still visible. The remaining letters have worn away.

I put down my coffee cup and look at the tag intently.

And then, before I can think about it anymore, before I can talk myself out of it yet again, I rub the tag between thumb and forefinger. And I whisper, "It's time to go, Scooter."

And this time, as the tears come once again to my eyes, I add, "I love you, Scooter."

I can only hope that will help him on his last run.

STORY NOTES

I AM NOT A fast writer, as a rule. Twice, I have ignored that rule and banged out something I've been really happy with quickly.

The second time was when I wrote the final novel in my *Aphotic* series, *FLESH AND BLOOD*, in the span of about three months, when it typically takes me a solid year or more.

The first time, however, was when I wrote two short stories in rapid succession—and I mean two stories in three days—for submission to a short story contest. I don't know which one I wrote first, but one of them was *Stealing Corey* (also in this collection) and the other was this one. I was happy with both of them, but this was my favourite of the two.

Why? Oh, the usual story…this one really happened. Fair warning: you'll read that a lot about the stories in these collections. "It really happened."

Okay, well, not everything in the story happened. But I did have a black lab with a white spot on one of his toes. I called him Dino after both the Flintstones's pet dinosaur and after Dean Martin, who I thought was hilarious.

Right up to the point where Scooter comes back, it's pretty accurate. Everything after that, I made up.

Here's an easter egg for you. The house I describe here with the pond and the magical woods that we had to give up? It's the same house and the same dog that I talk about in the story *Monster* (in *UGLY STORIES, VOL. 2*).

I kind of love this kind of writing, taking a whole episode from my life, and turning it into a fictional story. It sure as hell makes the writing easier.

Anyway, I got both stories completed, I submitted both to the competition. *Corey* was the one that got selected for that competition. That left me with a free story hanging around, looking for a home.

Flash forward about a year, and a very good friend of mine—and fellow author Pat Flewwelling—was having a book release in Montreal. I made the four-hour drive to attend and we were in a cool little restaurant/café. At one point, I got talking to a well-known Canadian author and anthology editor who happened to mention they needed a couple more stories for a new anthology to be called *EXPIRATION DATE*…

And Scooter immediately popped into my head. I drove back home that night and immediately submitted the story to the editor.

I will say, when the editor got back to me, they didn't seem remarkably impressed with the story, but did agree that it was good enough to have a place in the anthology. The editor made very few changes, with the exception of highlighting the "prison break" aspect of Scooter running away, then changing the title to one I detested: *Prison Break*.

Still, with an offer to publish on the table, and no fundamental changes happening beyond the title, I wasn't going to be precious about it.

(However, I also disliked that title so much that I went back to my original title for this collection).

The following year, I got a really good compliment on that story from an unexpected source. In 2016, in Ellen Datlow's *THE BEST HORROR OF THE YEAR, VOLUME EIGHT*, in her summation for 2015 horror anthologies, she wrote:

"*Expiration Date*, edited by Nancy Kilpatrick (Edge) includes twenty-five all-new stories about death and dying. The strongest is by Tobin Elliott, and two collaborations, one by Judith and Garfield Reeve-Stevens and the second by Steve Rasnic Tem and Melanie Tem."

And honestly, to this day, if I ever doubt myself, I flip to page XX (no, really, it's XX because that's the section where the pages are numbered Roman Numeral style) of that Best Of collection and I re-read that paragraph.

I mean, I don't necessarily agree that mine was in the top three (though Datlow is absolutely bang on about the one by the Judith and Garfield), it's just really cool that someone of Ellen Datlow's experience believes it to be so.

And it's also cool that I have a story that immortalizes my very first pet, too.

ANGEL

THERE ARE OTHERS who need my attention, but they would have to wait.

The hospital room is as shadowed as my thoughts. Presently, three of the four beds are unoccupied, which makes my job a little easier. But the room is too quiet. Lifeless. No broken-hearted relatives with their balled-up wads of tissues muttering the same old insipid lies:

"Everything is fine at home."

"It's gonna be okay."

Or the best: "You look great."

How many times have I heard these?

I turn my attention back to the lone occupied bed.

To the patient.

The venetian blinds cut the sunlight into thin strips on the bedsheets, and make the bandages seem to glow in the relative gloom. Too much light hurts her eyes.

Her.

The broken mass of tissue and bone before me. She was probably very pretty once, but that is gone. There are no more than a few square inches of flesh that remains unbruised. There are very few teeth left. Large patches of missing hair . Her nose is gone.

So is her virginity.

She is fifteen years old.

She'd run away from home two months before, with no warning. Just a few clothes and her favourite teddy bear were missing. The police were no help, having seen variations of this case hundreds of times.

Only two months? She's probably hooking and using in some large city by now. An old pro.

For two months, no one knew where she was. Her parents were frantic.

Then two days ago, her dad is getting in late from work, and finds her on the front steps. He thinks it's a bum, until he rolls her over. Almost unrecognizable, except for the teddy bear.

And now, Mom and Dad are never away from her side. She has never regained consciousness. She never will.

They will never get the chance to make her understand how much they love her. How they will never give up until the animal that did this to her is caught and punished.

God, what was done to her. Their baby. Their little girl.

How many times have I seen this?

♦♦♦

SHE IS DYING. It will not be long now.

And me. I can't do a damn thing, except stand here, unseen, delaying the inevitable. Others need me, there are too many hands on my time, but this one.... I can't seem to let her go. She should be dead by now.

But I don't want to let her go.

We wait for a time, the four of us. The sound of the machines beeping and breathing. Her parents softly sobbing. The sick smell of the institution. Walls green and peeling. The strips of light sliding silently across the sheets.

How many times have I been here?

It's times like this that I wonder, *why are you just sitting there? Why are you not talking to her? Singing to her? Touching her? She* knows *you are here. She* knows. *She* needs *this.* But they only sit there, watching the floor. They count the seconds, each breath from her body another guilty moment they still have with her.

Finally, I can wait no longer. I move to the bed, careful not to disturb her, or cause her more pain. Her parents do not notice, so wrapped are they in their own tombs of grief.

Carefully, oh so carefully, I slowly reach down to her breast. I take a deep breath, and reach farther. Farther. My long fingers reaching deep inside her, her warmth on my skin. Her breathing hitches slightly, then calms again. My hand is in her now, and then I find it. Her soul. My hand closes gently on it as I shut my eyes and prepare for the rush of images...

How many times have I done this?

"YOU LITTLE CUNT. You're gonna give me what I want. You're gonna give it and you're gonna give it now."

punches
kicks
and pain
worlds of pain
hitting my face
no
a hammer
hair in my mouth
his chest flexing as he pushes into me
ripping tearing
metal taste in my mouth
pliers
then dark
quiet

blood

pain

so much pain

worlds of pain

then confusion and cold and dark and pain and shame and guilt and hate and pain and desperation and dark and quiet and light and pain and hunger and hurt and shame and confusion and

...why, Daddy?...

How many times have I heard this?

AND MY HAND is out, and her soul is mine.

The room explodes in activity. Doctors and nurses yelling, machines wailing, more machines brought in, people shouting, all in a futile attempt to get back what is already gone. I wipe the tears from my eyes and back away from her. I have taken what made her alive.

I have taken her pain. A small blessing.

She is gone now.

Anything that she once was is gone.

She was brightness and light.

It's gone.

She was joy and happiness.

It's gone.

She was dreams and ambitions.

They're gone.

She was love and hate.

They're gone.

She was endless possibility and potential.

It's gone.

That was all gone before I arrived. I took the thing that kept her alive. But he...he took her life. In the corner of an abandoned factory. For two months.

Her father. I move to him, my hands shaking. I reach out to his breast.

There are rules against this.

I reach farther. His breathing hitches and his pupils flare. My hands curl around his essence. His eyes search frantically and he almost sees me.

A natural order of things that cannot be changed.

I touch his soul. I clench my teeth. I curse his existence.

But I pull back my hand.

His time is not now, but soon. Not soon enough. When it comes, it will be painful. A world of unending pain and hurt. And he will know why. I will be there.

I am the Angel of Death.

How many times must this happen?

STORY NOTES

YEAH, I KNOW this is nowhere near my best work. Probably not even near the middle.

I believe this may have been the second story—after *The Riff* (in *UGLY STORIES, VOL. 2*)—that I wrote to start fulfilling my 1996 New Year's Resolution (see my notes after *The Riff* for the full story…or not). I can still remember writing this one, thinking it was the greatest thing that'd ever been written. I saved the file, and didn't look at it for a week. Then, when I came back and read it again, I can remember thinking, *oh my god, this is shit.*

I couldn't even tell you why I kept it, but I'm kind of glad I did, though I'm still leaning more toward the shit ranking, to be honest.

It's that hackneyed, obvious story that I think a lot of beginning writers have to write if for no other reason than to just get it out of their system. I'm not saying everyone has an Avenging Angel of Death, but more the story of the person who was wronged, the one who did the wrongdoing, and how they got—or will get—their comeuppance.

Hell, it's about every third story that ever appeared in those pre-Comics Code comics, *Eerie* and *Creepy* and *Vault of Horror* and *Haunt of Fear*. It's a story that's been told over and over and over again.

And here comes Tobin to trod down that path that so many authors walked down before me, and made the trip far more successfully.

Still, I include it because it's a harbinger of things to come.

It's got a lot of elements that I'll pick at like scabs in my future fiction. After all, I am the guy who says he writes *ugly stories about terrible people doing horrible things*. Hell, I even name my collections with that phrase.

As Alice sings, *welcome to my nightmare.*

Here, you'll find a Very Bad Person hiding in plain sight. You'll find the Unsuspecting Victim who gets broken. You'll find a Supernatural Force who's either unsure of their ability, or somehow hampered from using it. And running through it, a rage that these things happen. All things that I return to on occasion.

So, yeah, I don't think this is an award winner, or anything particularly special, but if you look closely, you'll see the signposts that point toward the stuff that would show up almost thirty years later.

THE WRONG CHILD

DIANE'S EYES SNAPPED open, then, panicked, quickly checked the clock above the television. Suppertime. The house was far too quiet. And Glen would be home soon.

"Cassie?" A quick run through the house told her what the fluttering in her chest had said all along. Cassie wasn't home yet.

Frantic calls to Cassie's friends confirmed she hadn't got sidetracked on the way home. Diane threw some items into a diaper bag, scooped Cassie's baby sister Alex out of the crib where she had still been sleeping and, with Alex yowling at the sudden awakening, dropped her off next door with growly Mrs. Kovacs.

It took five stabs at the ignition before Diane slid the key home.

She stopped, dropped her head to the steering wheel and took a bunch of deep breaths. If she didn't calm herself, she'd never find her daughter. She'd wrap the car around a tree or something. A couple more deep breaths, then she twisted the key, thanking Glen for taking the fifteen-year-old Volkswagen Bug to work and leaving her the '69 Impala. They had wanted to buy new, but could only afford something a couple of years old, still it was much more dependable.

The big motor fired immediately and she dropped the car into gear.

Damn her! Cassie knew better than this. She always came straight home from kindergarten. Always. *Oh God, she's got to be all right. Please let her be all right.*

Damn, damn, DAMN! Mrs. Kovacs hadn't said anything to her when she dropped Alex off, her mouth squeezed down to a tight little sphincter as usual, but her silence was clear: *"Cassie's been missing over two and a half hours, and you're just noticing* now?" Mrs. Kovacs just didn't know how tired she was. Alex was just four months old, and Cassie...Cassie was a wrecking crew.

So when Alex went down for her nap, she was just going to rest on the couch for a bit and watch some of that newer soap *All My Children*—she always saw some similarities between herself and Mona Kane, a single mother just like her, bringing up that spoiled brat Erica—and her last thought was her hope that Cassie and Alex wouldn't grow up like one of those Pine Valley kids ... and then it was ten after six, no supper made, Cassie missing, and Alex with a dirty diaper.

Mrs. Kovacs was probably calling the police on her right now.

CASSIE SAT ON a bed of coppery gold pine needles under the tree. The branches drooped so low nobody could see in, but she could see out. She took a deep breath. She loved the smell in here. Not like her sister. She stunk. Like poo.

Things hadn't been the same since Alex came home with Mommy. Now Mommy told her to be quiet all the time, or to go play with her sister because Mommy was too tired. And Daddy, well he used to play with Cassie all the time, until Alex came...and then Daddy just stopped. Nobody said nothing, but Cassie knew why Daddy stopped.

Alex was why.

Alex ate up all their time. Mommy and Daddy had no time for her anymore. Just Alex.

All Alex could do was goober. And poop. And cry, cry, cry!

Nope. Cassie didn't like her at all. Just like she didn't like her Unca Charlie. He used to kiss her too much. And make her sit on his lap. And he smelled bad too. Just not like poo. But Unca Charlie used to make her feel funny and bad inside and she didn't like it and she didn't like him neither.

Lucky that was when she found out she could do things. She'd been able to –

A flicker of movement broke her thoughts.

Oh boy! A new playmate? She could try out some more new stuff!

PANIC ROSE IN her throat like an animal struggling to get itself loose. Half an hour and nothing. She'd even tried the schoolyard.

She wasn't there either.

The next place would be the park. She was probably there. She had to be there. *Oh Jesus, what if she wasn't there? What if somebody came and...*

No dammit. She was fine. Her baby was fine. She would find her on the swings, and she would smack her butt so hard...

But first she would kiss her and hug her and tell her how much she loved her.

CASSIE WATCHED THE big, black squirrel. It did that weird run-stop-run thing. Why did they do that? Like someone kept turning a switch on and off. *Click, click.*

It must have been gathering nuts for winter. Its cheeks bulged out, big and round, just like her Unca Charlie's. But he's dead now.

She wondered if she could get Mr. Squirrel to come over and play with her. She sure would like to pet that big twitchy fluffy tail.

She squinted her eyes to slits, and clenched her tiny fists tight. Almost tight enough to draw blood. Just like she had with Unca Charlie.

Mis-ter Squir-rel.

♦ ♦ ♦

"CASSIE. CASS?" DIANE didn't like the shrillness in her voice, but couldn't seem to keep it away. "C'mon baby, Mommy's not mad. Mommy just wants you home. Cassie? Honey?"

The evening air felt cold on her face. Not biting yet, but close. Snow would be here soon; she could smell it. The wind blew her long hair into her face. Leaves skittered playfully about her feet, as if dancing to a happy tune.

She pulled her sweater tighter around her. Christ, what kind of mother was she? She couldn't even remember if Cassie took her jacket this morning. She shivered violently.

"Cass?"

♦ ♦ ♦

MR. SQUIRREL WAS still doing his stop-start-stop hop. Cassie reached out and *pulled.* In mid-hop, he froze, then slowly lost his balance and toppled to the side, his little body heaving.

Ever since Unca Charlie got her real mad, she'd figured out she could do lots of stuff now. She'd been getting better at it a long time now, maybe since summer started, and that was years ago!

She remembered sitting in the playroom—Daddy called it a rumpus room, but that sounded like a room for a bum to Cassie—and she was thinking about how Unca Charlie would always make her sit on his lap and bounce her against his hard thing. Then he would breathe all funny and go all red in the face. Only then would he let her down and give her a dollar. She liked the dollar, but she hated Unca Charlie. But with Mommy all fat and preggers, no one seemed to have time for Cassie. And then Alex came. And then Mommy and Daddy kind of forgot about her.

But then, one time, Unca Charlie made her sit on his lap again, and he wouldn't let her go. He squeezed her, then he kissed her on the ear with his fat lips.

And Cassie got *mad.* So mad, she squinched her eyes and squeezed her fists. She felt weird then.

Not weird like Unca Charlie made her feel.

Different weird.

Good weird.

She made it so Unca Charlie would never bounce her or kiss her ever again. Maybe it had been a bad thing to do, because when she got down off his lap, everyone started paying lots of attention to him.

Maybe it had been bad, but that good weird? Yeah, it helped her to figure out what to do for Unca Charlie. And that wasn't bad, was it?

She'd learned to do other good weird stuff since then. And now, she had fluffy Mr. Squirrel to try stuff on!

Cassie focused on Mr. Squirrel again, and made him stand up and drop all the stuff in his mouth. Wouldn't want him to choke. Then she made him come over to the tree where she sat. Mr. Squirrel wasn't doing that stop-and-go thing anymore. He just walked over, but kind of shaky-like. Sort of like her toy doggy at home. But Mr. Squirrel didn't bark. Only doggies barked.

SHE ENTERED THE park just as the sky was darkening. Glen would be home soon. What the hell was she going to tell him? *"Here's your*

dinner. Oh, by the way, I lost Cassie." Oh, Jesus. She was losing it. Her kid, *and* her mind.

♦♦♦

THE SQUIRREL'S MIND was white with fear. His heart was pounding. She knew it. She knew when the heart went *bobbity bobbity bobbity*, it's was much too fast. The Kelly's cat Dammit had dropped dead when his heart did that. She couldn't get Dammit to do anything after that had happened.

So she slowed Mr. Squirrel's heart down, but not too much. She knew what happened when you did that too.

♦♦♦

THE SWINGS AND monkeybars were on the far side of the park, by the big old pine trees. She didn't see anyone, but it was a ways off. Cassie could be lying on the grass, watching the leaves, or maybe lying on her back with her dress up around her waist, and her underwear...

Diane heard a high quick scream that abruptly cut off. She started to run. The leaves swished and danced and whispered secrets she didn't want to hear.

♦♦♦

MR. SQUIRREL'S EYES rolled up in his head. He kept jerking like a dog on a leash. Cassie was having trouble controlling him. He wasn't being very much fun. But he was so cute! She forced him to climb up onto her lap, then she reached down to stroke his pretty tail. She'd never pet a squirrel before. It was going to be so soft, she could just tell. He was *sooo* pretty.

The squirrel spun and snapped at her hand.

"CASSIE? CASSIE! Omigodcassiewhere*ARE*you?"

"Mommy? I'm in here, Mom."

She was screaming Cassie's name so loud she almost missed it. But it was her. Cassie. Her baby was all right!

Frantically, she pushed her way through the sagging pine. The first thing that hit her was the smell.

"Mr. Squirrel's dead, Mom."

An animal's entrails were strewn all over the pine carpet. Everywhere. Steaming in the cool evening air.

But Cassie, there was nothing on her. There was no blood on her. Her baby was fine. She sobbed as Cassie stood and came into her open arms. Her pretty pink dress that Grandma gave her for Christmas last year had pine gum on it and she smelled of the mess on the ground. She hugged Cassie tight. Almost too tight. Cassie started to squirm. She put her down.

"He was my friend, Mommy. But now he's dead."

"Yes he is honey, and if you ever pull a stunt like this again, your daddy's probably going to kill us both." It was something that she regretted saying almost instantly. She softened her voice. "C'mon, baby, let's get home."

Cassie looked back to the tree. Mr. Squirrel was in there. Now he was bird food. He had been bad, and so she had punished him.

And that was the only part that had been fun. When she had made his pretty tail come out of his mouth, the squirrel had let out a short, high, *loud* scream. She didn't know anything could make a sound like that.

But then, she had never turned anything inside out before.

Anyway, she was going to try playing with Alex. Mommy was always telling her to. Besides, she could probably get Alex to do more things than some dumb old squirrel. And Alex didn't have any teeth, so she couldn't bite...

STORY NOTES

AND NOW WE come to one of the most important stories I've ever written.

There's a far more detailed version in the Author's Note at the end of *BAD BLOOD*, the first in my six-book Aphotic series.

So, I still officially credit *The Riff* as my first stab at seriously trying to write. Before this, back in the Seventies (senior public and high school) and the Eighties (working dead end jobs), I occasionally tried writing some stuff. A couple of very forgettable stories that actually never got finished. One that I'd started but would come back to later and call it *Horse Guts Horse Guts* (in UGLY *STORIES, VOL. 2)*, even the start of a novel that, to this day still scratches a little at my writer's brain...

...there's still a kernel of some cool story in there somewhere and maybe I'll crack it one day...

...and then there was this one. I started this one when I was a manager at Arby's, so, call it 1983 or 84.

I started it, yes, but never quite finished it. Didn't know what the hell to do with a kid that was basically a nine-year-old Carrie White.

When I started getting serious about the writing thing in the latter half of the Nineties, somewhere along the lines, I stumbled across some old three-ringed binder papers with half-done stories on them in my neat printing.

This was the one that grabbed me. I think I'd had her to the point where she was under the tree and saw a squirrel. That was it. Obviously, I might have had some idea back in the early Eighties of where I was planning on going with it, but by the late Nineties, I had no clue what younger Tobin had been planning.

Didn't matter. I knew exactly what I was going to do with that poor little squirrel. And I also knew exactly how to end it.

Long story short, I cleaned up the first half, completed the second half, and filed it away, reasonably happy with the story, never happy with the title.

Then, ten years later, when my novel deal got pushed back and the publisher asked if I could write a short lead-in to the novel, something to whet the appetite, I initially thought, *nope, I got nothing.*

Then I remembered a little girl and a squirrel.

And it was the start of an entire series. I just didn't know it at the time.

Started in the 1980s.

Finished in the 1990s.

Repurposed in the late 2000s.

Initially published in the early 2010s

Rejigged and published, starting a series in the 2020s.

One story, forty years in the making.

Sometimes it takes decades for that lightning to strike, doesn't it?

STEALING COREY

I JUST WANNA leave a mark, y'know?"

He scooped up a handful of sand. Only the two of us at the beach this time of night. The moonlight slid like mercury over the waves as they hissed toward us.

Corey contemplated the sand as he leaned against the car. Then his fingers closed and his hand tilted sideways. The sand cascaded out like an hourglass.

"I just see my mom, my relatives, our teachers..." The sand slid from his hand. "They get so caught up in life they forget to live, y'know?" The sand continued falling, a conical mound between his knees.

The sand ran out, the last few grains trickling from his palm. He turned to me.

"I don't ever want to not *live*."

♦ ♦ ♦

STEALING COREY'S ASHES is easier than I thought it would be.

I sneak out through the Jones's kitchen and then through the patio doors. Initially, I'm not sure if Corey's mother sees me or not, but I figure she'd think I was heading out for a smoke.

With Corey dead three days, who the hell knows what she's thinking?

For a brief moment, just before I close the sliding glass door, I stop to look at her, alone in a room full of people, leaning against the dining room table, a paper plate of food drooping at a hazardous angle. Even with her eyes staring vacantly at a section of carpet, the plate forgotten in her hand, there's still something about her. A nobility, I guess.

The same nobility I sensed when Corey first entered that classroom three years ago.

♦♦♦

I SHOWED UP in grad ten, the obvious new kid. To call me awkward would have been a kindness.

I was that strange kid that rattles around every classroom in every school, mostly ignored, often derided. The overly skinny boy with the acne and the glasses. The one who's clothes fit the hanger in the closet better than they fit him. The weird one. The square peg in school full of round holes.

It wasn't like I didn't know the words. I could speak human, I could fake the words and the feelings, but the words never seemed to fit my mouth right. They tumbled from me like I was spitting out golf balls.

It was easier to simply not talk. What's that quote? Something about letting others think you're a fool rather than opening your mouth and removing all doubt? That was me.

As I sat at a desk, idly doodling in my brand new binder, grinding my teeth, waiting for a teacher to arrive and put me out of my misery, every other student hung back. Eyeballing me. Finding me wanting.

Thinking me a fool.

Then he walked in. Nothing outwardly different about him, yet, there was an undefinable *something* about him. He waved to a few kids, his eyes roving the room.

I guess that's when he spotted me. The newbie.

With no hesitation, he walked straight over and, in an oddly adult move, stuck out his hand. I'd never seriously shaken hands with anyone in my life to that point, yet it felt oddly natural to put my hand out and clasp his.

"Corey Jones. You must be the new kid in town."

I knew I should say something, but for the life of me, I couldn't think of anything. So lost, I forgot to let go of his hand. He loosened his grip and I realized I'd held on too long. I dropped my hand, feeling the blush rising to blow any chance I had of escaping the shy kid curse. I realized my teeth were still ground together and forcibly unlocked them.

"Uh-huh..." I mumbled.

Out of the corner of my eye, I saw a few grins light up the eyeballers. I felt my face radiate more heat.

Corey looked down at my binder. "That Cyclops?" he said. "From the X-Men?"

I was stunned enough that I almost didn't answer. But I managed to get a weak "yeah" out. Thinking, *he's being kind.* Thinking, *he only knows Cyclops from the stupid movies.*

"Yeah, he's cool. That's a great comic book. Though I like his brother Alex more."

I glanced up at him and we both said "Havok" at the same time.

A nice guy *and* he read comics.

Then he leaned in a bit. Not a lot, but enough that it felt conspiratorial. "Hey," he said. I couldn't answer him. My throat tightened at the reaction of the others. I expected the smartass comment and dismissal that normally occurred right around this time.

I was just as awkward as I'd been signaling up to now.

"Hey," Corey said again. Then he leaned in closer still and clapped me on my bony shoulder. "Don't worry about them," he whispered, cocking his head in their direction. "They're rude to old people and they kick babies when their mamas aren't looking, just to hear them cry."

As a joke, it was so lame, yet it caught me by such surprise, I let a long, loud belly laugh go.

Then I told him my name and things got better from there.

NOW, LOOKING AT Mrs. Jones, Corey's ashes hidden behind my back, I watch as she lifts her dull, red-rimmed eyes to mine. They crinkle as she raises a weak smile but I see the pain etched in there.

Husband long gone, and now her only son dead.

I see how the rest of her life will go.

I come very close to opening that door again to replace Corey's urn.

But I don't.

BY THE TIME I get to the beach, it's dark. The moon once again sliding like mercury over the waves.

I sit in the sand, leaning against the car. The brushed surface of the urn shines dully under the moonlight.

"You know, Corey," I say, addressing the urn. "You never played a musical instrument. You couldn't sing or act. You didn't write much of anything unless it was assigned by a teacher, and even then, I wrote most of it. So you were never going to get famous that way, dude."

I run my hand through my hair.

"You were barely even a blip on social media. God, if someone wanted to friend you, they'd wait months for you to confirm. Even for me, and I was your best friend, you dick." I sigh.

"And yet, there was that *something* about you. Something I've never been able to define. Yet, I felt it from the first time we met."

This is normally where I'd tear up. I'd done it earlier at the funeral, and again when I talked to Corey's mother. Of course, there's no reason to do so now. Still, there's a strange, alien tug at my heart.

I crush the feeling and carry on.

I lift the top off the urn. All that is left of Corey is in there.

I pull a Ziploc bag out of my pocket and scoop some of Corey into it, seal it, hold it up to the light. This is all that's left of Corey. Ashes and dust. A poor reminder of something now past. I tuck the bag into a pocket.

Then I pick up a handful of sand. I contemplate it for a long time.

"In a very real way, Corey, you didn't really leave a mark." I close my hand over the sand. "I mean, how many teenagers ever do?"

I tilt my hand and the sand cascades out like an hourglass.

"And worse, you were starting to forget to live, buddy. You were beginning to lose that *something*. I saw it falling away from you."

I shift my hand slightly and the sand pours into the urn.

"It was your time," I say. The last of the sand trickles into the urn. "And Corey?"

"Maybe that's why we met. Maybe that's why we're friends. You helped me, now I help you."

I lean closer to the ashes and sand, conspiratorially. I whisper, "I just want you to know, because of me, you *will* leave a mark. Every time they think of me and hate me, they'll remember: *you* were my first." I pat the urn. "That's you, buddy. Someday, in the future, when they count my kills, your name will always be the first on the list. And no one can ever take that away from you."

I thank Corey one last time.

♦♦♦

I RISE FROM the ground, brushing sand from my pants, from the urn. I pat the bag tucked safely in my pocket.

I've got to go back to Corey's place, to return the urn.

But I also need to visit his mother. She's another who's forgotten how to live.

I think of her dull eyes, her lifeless face, and I know what I have to do.

STORY NOTES

THIS ONE WAS written in a burst with one other story, *Scooter's Last Run,* that opens this collection. The Scooter story was, like much of my writing, based on real events.

This one, however, was probably the first one that was inspired by a song.

I was—and I still am—a big Better Than Ezra fan. I've loved their stuff since the album *Deluxe* came out back in 1993. This story, however, has its roots in a song from their 2001 album, *Closer*. The fifth track, "A Lifetime" grabbed me. It's a song about a friend dying, passing away on the day of her graduation. Specifically, there were a couple of lines about the girl's mother not minding like he—the singer—thought she would.

I wasn't quite sure what the mother was not minding, but somehow, I got it in my head that it had something to do with the singer taking the girl's ashes for one last… I don't even know. One last drive? One last night on the town? One last visit to someplace that held special significance?

I will say, when I wrote the story initially, I wrote it straight. The guy takes his buddy's ashes and just tells him what their relationship meant to him, what he'd learned from it. It was a bittersweet ending.

Then, another writer friend of mine read it and, when she was done, kind of wrinkled her nose. "I liked it a lot until it got all syrupy at the end." Then she said, "You need to go darker with it."

So, I mulled it over for a bit, then I went darker. I'm glad I did. I like this ending far better.

This is why it's important to have readers who'll call you out on your shit. Thanks, Pat!

I submitted both this and the *Scooter's Last Run* story to a contest. This is the one that was accepted for the resulting anthology that's now long out of print.

Also, fun fact: this one is kinda sorta connected to *BLOOD LOSS*, the third book in the *Aphotic* series, if you squint your eyes and clamp your tongue between your lips at precisely the right angle. I won't spell it out directly, but I'll just leave this little hint here for anyone who cares to look: The narrator in this story doesn't have the affectation that would come later.

And on that note, I'll let it be.

PAST SINS, SINCE PAST

50

THERE WAS ALWAYS the same age difference between us. Thirty-five years.

It wouldn't be long now. I'd go soon. I had so many memories.

When one memory came, and then the next would add its weight to the first, then each successive remembrance attached itself, each adding its weight to the one before. A critical mass of memory. Of history.

Of pain.

That critical mass...I don't know if that was him calling to me, or me wanting to protect him.

When the memories became overpowering, I would reach into my wallet and pull out the small piece of paper. I'd read it over and over. I would re-examine the handwriting for any clue to what had been going through my head.

When I pulled out that piece of paper, I always knew it wouldn't be long.

When that happened, I visited him.

In the meantime, waiting for it to happen, I put the coffee on.

39

THE FIRST TIME, I stood in front of the house. It was late and it was dark. Darker than I'm used to thirty-five years later. Back then, not only were there no streetlights, there was also no omnipresent glow from the city. I stared into a field of black velvet, bejeweled with thousands of stars.

Stars I could no longer find today.

I stood, my gaze falling from the stars to our old house, now thirty-five years newer. I heard the sound of tires on gravel as I knew I would, and I saw our sky-blue '62 Pontiac rolling up the road. My God, the amount of chrome! And in the front, my father driving, my mother in the passenger seat, both of them younger than I am now.

Then the memory, like the remembrance of a first kiss, a double-backing of image on image. I knew I was in the back seat. I'd been sleeping but I would be awake now.

I'd be sitting up, sensing the slowing of the car, maybe the subtle change in my parents' voices. I would be pushing off the cold blue vinyl of the seat and...

And there I was, the top of my head rising.

I made eye contact with myself, thirty-five years earlier. I remember being that child, saying, "Mommy, who's that man?"

4

"MOMMY, WHO'S THAT man?"

We'd lived here a long time. I'd been born there, four years ago. And I'd never seen the man that stood near the tree, a little back from the road. It was weird, because he hung back in the shadow of the tree, but I could see him clearly. I can't explain it, but I wasn't *seeing* him like I saw everyone else. He stood out more. Seemed a little more real.

"What man, honey?" She had turned her head to look at me and her face was illuminated in the glow from the dashboard lights. I saw her eyes, her smile, the kind expression she always seemed to save just for me.

I lifted my hand to point, got so far as to say, "Right th—" But there was no one there.

"There's no one out there, honey," she said.

She was right.

But he *had* been.

And though it would be almost seven more years before I saw that strange, extra-real man again, I thought about him all the time.

46

AND THOUGH IT would be almost seven more years before I saw that strange, extra-real man again, I thought about him all the time.

The second time I went back, I was determined to do more than just stand and watch myself. Looking back on that, I laugh, because I knew very well how it turned out prior to even going back.

Still, we hope for the best, don't we?

I stood a little off from the cabin, facing the back of it. I heard the sounds of the kids around the other side, playing soccer. That damnable school trip I'd had to participate in.

My hand was in my jacket pocket, casual. In the other pocket, the familiar weight of a treasured friend as well as a replacement for the loss of an old friend. I knew what had been written on the first, still, somehow never written at all, yet somehow had always been written on it. It was simply my job to give both the new and the old ones to him. That's how it would be done. How it had always been done.

Then I saw myself—Leo—the younger me—walk into the area of the cabin where the bunks were. I knew he'd look around before he did what he did, so I backed into the trees where I wouldn't be seen. I didn't need to see what I did all those years ago. Once was enough.

Instead, I put my other hand in my pocket, felt the shape there. Riffled the edge. Thought about what it meant to me back then. What was written inside.

I let him do his thing. I waited, tense, knowing what was coming.

11

IN GRADE SIX, we had to go to a camp. School trip. For a week. Something about building my character. It came right in the middle of a crapload of change for me, when the last thing I needed to do was build character.

I didn't need any more change.

This coming June, my mother was going to marry Bob, who would become my new dad. By the end of the school year, I was going to have a new dad, I was going to be in a new house, I was going to be in a new school, I was going to have a new last name.

And now I had to go spend a week with a bunch of kids and teachers I either didn't like, or didn't know. Because I really had no friends.

My mom seemed so happy about this week away, prattling on about *how good it would be* for me, and I *would have such great experiences,* I would end up with *so many new memories*. She had these irritating phrases. So hopeful. So stupid.

And Bob, my incoming stepfather, completely agreed.

I knew none of it was true. But I didn't let on how much I dreaded it. I just shut up and dutifully packed for a week away. A week in hell.

When we were shown our cabin, we were made to stand outside with our bags, waiting for the teachers to unlock and set up the cabin. I hadn't really made any friends in my class. Tamara Wilson talked to me occasionally, but that was because I owned a pencil sharpener and she didn't, so she'd borrow it all the time. She sat in front of me in class, and she thought she was some kind of hot shit because her mother was a teacher at the school and it didn't help that she was really pretty, with her long, golden-brown hair and her green eyes that didn't just look at you, they kind of locked on to yours.

She always made me feel weird when she looked at me.

Anyway, she was the only one I really talked to and she, I believed, was the one responsible for saddling me with my first school nickname. *Oil.* She'd oh so brilliantly turned *Leo* around backward and pronounced it *Oil.* Of course it stuck.

And for all of that, I still would have preferred having her here to talk to. If only to lend a sharpener, or have her call me Oil. Instead, it was all boys, as was, in the words of my new, Glasgow-born stepfather, "right and fit and proper." I didn't know if that's how all people from Glasgow talked, but at times it made me want to puke.

When they allowed us access, the twenty or so boys ran like unbridled horses into the cabin to claim the best bed space. My needs were simpler. I just didn't want a top bunk. No particular reason other than me hating climbing up and down anytime I left the bed.

When I came in, I did a slow walk of the beds, and every damn one of them seemed to have been claimed. The best ones were the single units, pushed tight to the far walls. There were only two of them, four beds upper and lower. They'd likely been the first to go. The rest of the bunk units were pushed together in pairs, two upper and two lower, then the next set of two.

As I walked the room, it appeared there were absolutely no beds left, then, as I was ready to give up, there was one lower bunk seemingly unclaimed. I looked around, but there was no bag on the bed, under it. I gingerly dropped my bag on the bed.

"Oil loses!" one of the boys said.

I wanted to ask him what he meant, but I also didn't exactly want to know. Maybe the bed was short-sheeted. Maybe there was a dead squirrel under the covers. I didn't know, and decided I'd wait and find out later.

46

OIL. I'D FORGOTTEN that name. I fucking hated it. Still, to this day.

11

THE REST OF the day went relatively smoothly, considering. In fact, it wasn't until that evening that I began to understand how lousy this week was shaping up to become.

After dinner and clean up, we all had free time. The first order of business was to, as my uncle would say, "pinch a loaf." I grabbed the paperback I was reading, Martin Caidin's *Cyborg*, and headed to the washroom.

I'd just settled, found my place in the book, and began reading when I heard a noise. Came from above me.

When I looked up, I realized several things at once. The bunks at the very end butted up to one wall of the washroom. The top bunk allowed access over the top of the wall. And there was no ceiling to the bathroom.

But worse, one of the guys up there was Brad Steffen. I'd pretty much avoided him for the past three years, though he did manage to occasionally harass and bully me.

He was the one change I was looking forward to. When I changed schools, he would be out of my life.

I stared up in what I could only assume was a gobsmacked fashion, at five of my classmates, staring down. I never really understood the term gobsmacked when my stepfather used it. Until now.

"What the hell, guys?" I said.

Five grins broke into five snorting, jeering laughs. "What'sa matter, Oily?" Brad Steffen said. "Can't make poo-poos with an audience?"

"You weren't plannin' on pullin' yer pud, were ya?"

"Whatcha readin', Oil? That some kinda porno book?"

Then I saw Brad's mouth pooch up a bit. I didn't know what he was going to do until I saw the wad of spit fly out of his mouth. It hit my cheek and chin. Then, before I could even react, more gobs of spit came from above.

Though I still had to go, I quickly dropped the book and pulled up my pants, the moisture from their saliva darkly mottling the fabric of my jeans. I scooped the book and bolted for the door. Behind and above me, amid the laughter, I heard, "Ain'tcha gonna wash yer hands? That ain't sanitary, Oil!"

46

BRAD STEFFEN. THE Steffenwolf. Friend and foe. Seeming eternal tormenter and bane of my existence. Yet, all in the span of three years.

Three years was a long time when I wasn't even in my teens yet.

I didn't hate the guy. Not anymore.

I even stopped wondering what happened to him decades ago. But when I was eleven years old, my god. There were times when I truly wanted him dead.

And once, I'd gone too far in punishing him.

11

FACE BURNING WITH anger and embarrassment, I went back to my bunk. The principal of our school sat on the adjoining bed. "I guess we're bunkies," he said, pushing his glasses up his small rat face. Damn. Stuck beside the principal. The most uncool spot in the cabin.

My stomach roiled with the need to crap and with the understanding of exactly how this week was going to go. And because I now knew why Oil had lost.

46

REVISITING THIS EVENT thirty-five years later, I felt my stomach roil once again, in sympathy for that skinny little kid in the cabin. Acid burned the back of my throat. I knew what was coming.

11

OVER THE NEXT three days, I noticed two things. The first was, I couldn't enter that washroom without getting at least a three-head audience. The second was, everyone else in the cabin was exempt from this treatment.

I thought about telling one of the teachers, but then I would have lost all face. It was bad enough that I was Oil, worse that I couldn't piss or shit without someone cracking a joke. The worst would have been to be labelled a snitch in a cabin of twenty of my peers, with no escape.

So I shut my mouth and suffered in silence, even though the solution to my problem slept in the bunk right beside mine. I kept my mouth shut even when I came back to my bunk after one uneaten meal to find the cover of the novel I'd been reading. It had been laid neatly on my pillow. There were no pages in it at all anymore. When I opened my sleeping bag, I found the pages, all three hundred and some of them, balled up and scattered inside.

I stayed silent. I wouldn't give them the satisfaction of seeing the anger, the rage. I kept it all inside.

I found opportunities to break away from activities for a few moments to piss in different, less public accommodations, but it was four days before I could shit.

Those four days were an exercise in increasingly painful humiliation. On two occasions, I found a washroom that was private enough, but by then, when I sat down, I felt myself tense up and I could not empty myself, no matter how much I willed it.

Instead, I would sit on the toilet, silent tears of agony and rage dripping from my face, and beg my body to do what it needed to do. And each time, I would pull my pants back up and wipe my face, then leave.

By the third day, I stopped eating altogether.

By the fourth day, I could barely walk without doubling over from the pain. But I couldn't show any of this. The slightest show of discomfort brought knowing, malicious sniggers from my classmates. I suffered in silence, desperate for relief, but terrified of allowing myself to relax, only to be embarrassed yet again.

Even though I wasn't eating, I still had to sit at the long wooden benches, a plate of food in front of me I desperately wanted, but couldn't eat. I had to sit while those faces sat around me, sharing looks with each other, lording grins of triumph over me.

I was in agony.

My guts heaved and seethed.

I kept telling myself to just hold on until tomorrow. Tomorrow we went home. Tomorrow, I wouldn't have to worry about these assholes any more.

But that didn't work out the way I'd planned.

After dinner Thursday evening, I picked up my untouched plate and walked it dutifully back to the kitchen, scraped it into the garbage can, stacked the plates beside the sink, the glass in the holder, the fork, knife and spoon in the plastic tub. All I wanted to do was go lay down on my bed. Maybe try to read. Then I remembered I didn't have a book anymore.

Instead, as I headed out of the kitchen, I felt a hand on my shoulder. "Whoa, whoa, whoa," one of the teachers said. "Where you think you're going, Oi—Leo?"

I'd never heard one of the teachers use my nickname before this. I kept my face neutral, pretending to not notice. But all I could think was, *Fucker fucker fucker!* Still, my voice was calm as I said, "Just back to my bunk, I guess."

"After you finish washing up."

I stared at him blankly. His sideburns, large wedges that rode his head almost to his jawline, bobbed in and out as his muscles worked.

"You're on duty tonight." His arm gestured at the counters of the kitchen, taking in the stacks of pots, pans and dishes. "This stuff isn't going to wash itself. It's your turn. You and..." he leaned forward to a sheet of paper tacked on the wall. "You and Steffen."

"Right here," said Brad. He'd been standing off to the side. He gave me a smile and a nod.

My heart sank.

"Okay," I said. I thought, *Fuck me.*

46

I REMEMBER WE took care of the dishes mostly in silence, Steffen saying nothing once the teacher left. That worked for me, because I remember it hurt just to stand up. I took the washing chore, partly because everyone wants to dry, and I figured if I took the shittier job, Steffen might be a bit happier. But I also took it because it meant I could pretty much stand in one spot and not have to walk around. That way, the concrete cinder block in my bowels wouldn't get knocked around as much.

Why? Why did I always take the shittier jobs? God, I wanted to just take that poor little bastard that was the younger, more stupid me and tell him not to do that anymore. Just that.

But, of course, I couldn't, could I?

Watching him, seeing the pain on his face, I remember thinking, *just get through the plates.* Then, *just get through the glasses.* Then the utensils. The pots and pans were the toughest, but when they were done, it was a quick wipe down of the counters and we'd be out.

It took everything in my forty-six-year-old body to not go in and help him. Or to not go in there and crack Steffen over the head. I'd never forgotten what came next.

It took the better part of an hour. In that hour, as I watched him, he might have said four words to Steffen. And I remember being slightly aware of it at the time, but seeing it now, I caught every one of the sarcastic grins, the faces, the sidelong glances he tossed my way. The eleven-year-old me ignored them all. *Just get through it.*

11

I GAVE THE counters the final swipe, and draped the dishcloth over the kitchen faucet to dry. I let out a breath. I could go back to my bunk. The simple relief of that thought almost brought me to tears.

I turned.

Brad stood there.

"What?" I said. I thought, *Don't cry. Just don't cry.* I did everything I could to mask how much his additional bulk intimidated me. Why was he doing this? Why were they doing this?

"Nothin'," he said.

I tried to push by him, but he easily outweighed me. I couldn't move him. He pushed me back, and pain arced from my bowels to my chest.

He saw the pain on my face. A slow grin slid across his face, stretching the thin, but clearly visible beginnings of a mustache and chin hair.

"How's the tummy, Oil?"

"Shut up," I said to my former friend. *Why had I ever stolen that stupid car? Why had I never returned it to him?*

"You know, I've heard a few people say you're fulla shit, Oil." The grin spread wider. "I gotta say, I think they're right."

Then he punched me, just once, below the belt, in my abdomen.

I dropped to my knees, tears first flooding, then sliding from my eyes. My arms encircled my stomach. Brad walked away laughing. Another great story for his friends.

46

STANDING OUTSIDE THE cabin, I saw the two of them. I saw Brad, well on his way to manhood, move forward, remembered the punch. I remembered exactly what had happened, and clutched at my own belly, as though I could feel that punch thirty-five years later. I couldn't feel it, but the memory burned. I remembered it with clear-eyed intensity. Anger and hate boiled up in me worse now, thirty-five years later, than it did in that kid inside the cabin. And still, I could do nothing.

I never had been able to do much. But he would take care of that part. Soon.

I gave the younger me time. I remember it took a lot for me to drag myself back to a standing position, and even then, I needed the support of a wall to keep me standing. The pain kept me doubled over. My entire midsection went cold. It felt like my asshole was just going to drop off and release everything—shit, guts, everything—inside me.

Staring at that cabin, I saw only the inside. My hand on the wall as my first step blew a gasp out of me. After that, I took small sips of air, released them slowly. Then I turned my attention to getting out of the kitchen, through the dining hall, down the hall and to the washroom.

I remember thinking, *Audience or not, I need to go. Fuck them if they wanna watch.*

11

MY MIDSECTION FELT like it was filled with cold, wet concrete and someone was trying to pour more in.

I took the path through the dining hall as fast as I could. It seemed to stretch for miles. I forced myself forward, still sipping air, swiping at the tears that kept welling in my eyes. One step. Two. It seemed to take hours. Eventually, years later, I stood at the corner where the dining room met the hallway.

I looked at the washroom, miles, leagues away. I saw the doorway halfway down the hall that led to the bunks.

Then I saw someone come through it. I ducked painfully back around the corner. I heard him say something, but couldn't make it out.

Then someone else came into the hall. They were discussing...what?

Soccer.

They were going to play soccer.

In a rush, everyone piled out of the cabin. I saw them through one of the large-paned windows. I thought, *I'm seeing them through panes of glass and through pain.*

I did a quick count, and got the right number of kids, but it took three tries. Hard to count when they're running around like that.

If I had it right, there was no one in the cabin.

Ignoring the pain, I rushed down the hall, but I had to stop at the doorway to the bunks. The throbbing, searing jabs in my guts doubled me over. I didn't know if I was going to make it.

Then I changed my mind and turned in toward the bunks.

46

WHEN HE FINISHED, I moved forward and waved him out. I had something for him.

11

WHEN I FINISHED, I hopped from the bunk and looked around. Then I saw a motion through one of the windows that looked out the back of the cabin, the opposite side to the soccer playing assholes.

Someone was out there.

He looked familiar.

He waved frantically at me to come out.

Shit! He'd seen me! Even worse: *How long had he been watching?*

I didn't know what to do. Looking at him, I didn't sense anger, or judgment, or danger. I had no idea how I got that from him, but I did. Enough to overcome my reluctance at going out to meet someone that had theoretically watched me…do what I did.

I ducked around out the doorway back to the hall, back through the dining room and to the kitchen where I exited through the cabin's back door.

He was gone.

I looked around and didn't see him anywhere, but I saw something on the ground. A white, rectangular shape. Small.

When I walked over and bent to look at it, it was the size of a really thick book.

Somehow, I'd expected it to be *Cyborg* by Martin Caidin. The ones those assholes had destroyed.

My curiosity got the best of me. I picked it up and unwrapped it, and damned if it wasn't *Cyborg*…but there was another book behind it.

The second book was a little beaten up, obviously handled and read, the spine broken, but it was in one piece. There was even a bookmark slid between the pages, right at the front pages of the book.

There was no writing on the cover. Just a girl's face, half in shadow. No title or author. Above the illustration were the words, *A novel of a girl possessed of a terrifying power.*

The bookmark was a simple piece of lined paper, torn from a notebook, but there was a message written on it. The handwriting looked familiar. I'd get back to the note in a minute, because there was something else written in the book itself in the same handwriting.

It said,

Leo,

I see you through panes of glass and through pains long past.

Read this book and know there's hope. When you're bullied, remember, others pay for their sins.

Karma's a bitch.

On the bookmark was a quicker, scrawled note. It looked like it had been done last minute. Weirdly, the scrawled note looked almost like something I could have written. I was about to read it as I heard the first scream from the cabin. I walked a few paces farther, so I was out of sight of the cabin, hidden by some trees, but I could plainly hear through the open windows.

It was Brad Steffen.

"Who the fuck shit on our beds?" Then, "Fucking Oil!"

I was likely going to get beaten for pinching a loaf on each of the onlooker's sleeping bags, but at this point, I didn't even care. It had been worth it. And they'd been runny.

As much pain as I'd been in, I hadn't been able to stop giggling as I did it.

Now a little more hidden, I looked down at the note again. It said,

Way to give them shit!

I guffawed at that. Then I ran like hell down a path and away from the cabin.

When I was far enough from the cabin to relax, I looked closer at the book. The page the sheet of paper marked was the gobbledygook about publishing and stuff that I never really looked at before. But this time, for some reason I did.

It said,

Copyright © 1974 by Stephen King

which was no big deal. It was the words a little ways down that caught me.

First Printing, April, 1975

Which was six months from now.

I looked back to what had been written inside, realizing I'd thought something similar only minutes earlier.

I see you through panes of glass and pains long past.

46

I DID END up paying for what I did to Brad.

Then again, I made him pay, too, didn't I?

15

THE OLD GUY stood a little way down the highway, pinging a memory from when I was a little kid, in the back of my parents' 62 Pontiac. It had been night back then, unlike the bright afternoon of now.

He didn't have his thumb out, so he wasn't a hitchhiker, but he wasn't walking either. He could have been taking a break from either, but that wasn't the sense I got. He didn't ping my mother's radar as she left the small, two-lane highway and angled the big Suburban along the hill where our long, winding driveway ran. She hadn't noticed how intently he stared into the car as we passed out of view into our wooded lot. She didn't notice him at all. And I didn't say anything about him.

Though, to be honest, just seeing him gave me chills.

It'd been about four years since I'd last seen him.

We got out of the car and Mom turned to head inside. I tried to keep my voice even. "I'm gonna go up and check the mail, okay?" I said. "Maybe take Deena for a walk?"

She turned back to me and smiled. "Okay." Checking her watch, she said, "Be inside by five for dinner, okay? If you have some time, you could bring in some more firewood." She grinned, knowing how well that would go over. I hated bringing in more firewood to the box in our foyer. I only did it so my stepfather wouldn't rip me a new asshole. Nice enough guy, but that was a particular issue for him. Then again, these days, everything I did seemed to be an issue for him.

Maybe not so nice a guy.

"Okay," I said. I tried to put the appropriate amount of chagrin in my expression, because all I wanted to do was get to the road to see if the guy was there.

"Hold on, let me let Deena out."

She seemed to take forever to get inside, but she finally did, held the door open, and Deena, my Golden Lab, ran out, full of boundless energy and delighted to see me. The two of us ran back along the quarter-mile driveway.

He was still there.

He beckoned me over with a motion that I recognized. I know that sounds weird because anyone that hooks their arm and drags it toward themselves is obviously beckoning. But it was the way he did it.

Most people will just swing their arm. He did too, but he also waggled his fingers. I hadn't seen anyone else do that.

Well, anyone else besides me.

So, he beckoned me with that odd, finger-waggling motion. Then he smiled.

I slowed. *Wow. He sort of reminds me of—*

Then Deena ran up to him, delighted to see him. He seemed equally delighted to see her.

He dropped to his haunches and held his arms out—again, eerily like I usually did when I got home to my dog—then a wide grin split his face and he said, "Oh my god, *Pasadeena*! C'mere, girl!"

And she did. My dog did.

And that actually stopped me in my tracks.

No one called my dog "Pasadeena" except me. Her name was Deena, and it was just a stupid nickname I'd picked up along the way.

I watched as he scrubbed at her ruff, and her ears, and she whined happily and licked at his face. His eyes lifted from the dog to me, and he briefly closed them, as though he was in some pain. With one last scratch behind her ear, the guy stood again. Deena, the little traitor, turned to face me, dropped her butt and sat down beside him, tongue lolling.

What the hell?

I approached him cautiously. Sure, I was damn near the same height as him...but I was only fifteen. Up until recently, kids my own age regularly got the drop on me, so I wasn't about to get near some old guy so he could do the same thing. Besides, this was the Seventies. There was some weird shit happening in the world. I didn't need to be picked up by the next Charlie Manson or get dragged into some whacky cult. I'd heard about them and they freaked me out.

So, I approached him, but I kept a healthy distance between us.

"Hey Leo," he said.

I stopped for the second time. "How do you know my name?" I said.

His face got strange then. I guess there was a bit of sadness in it. Nothing creepy, but still, it changed.

"That's a long story."

"You know my parents?" I said.

He looked up and the corners of his mouth lifted. He let out a short, clipped huff that could have been a laugh or almost a snort. "Yes," he said. "I know your mother, your stepfather, and your dad very well."

My dad. I hadn't seen Dad in a few years.

Okay, well, that's a lie.

14

A YEAR BEFORE we moved to New Hope, I ran into my father. Well, to be technical, *he* actually ran into me. I didn't often ride my bike downtown, but there was a great bookstore there that I visited at least once a month. The *Good Books and Magazine Store*. They fed my growing addiction to comics and science fiction novels. And horror novels, of course. Ever since I'd read *Carrie*, given to me during that hellish week at camp.

I see you through panes of glass and through pains long past.

There was a variety store just down the street from the book store, so when I did go there, I'd lock up my bike, check out the bookstore, then, before I was ready to head back, I'd pop into Mike's Place, a variety store with pool tables in the back and a permanent fug of cigarette smoke. I usually picked up a Pepsi, a Tahiti Treat, a Mountain Dew or, as a particular treat, a bottle of clear Cream Soda. Nothing made me burp as robustly as clear Cream Soda.

On this one particularly warm summer day, I locked my bike to a pole on the street and, anticipating the air conditioning and a cold Mountain Dew, ambled to the entrance for Mike's Place. Going through the door, I collided with somebody coming out. We hit hard enough to bounce off each other. When I looked up into the man's scowling face, I could tell he was drunk.

"The hell's the matter with ya, asshole?" he said. He pushed me out of the way and staggered down the street.

I stood, staring at him as he wobbled down the street. Granted, I hadn't seen him in almost five years, but still...

What man doesn't recognize his own son?

50

I GOT DOWN on my haunches, scratching Deena between her shoulders, just where she liked it. I hadn't seen her in so long, and yet, even in this fifty-year-old carcass, she still knew me. I hadn't realized how much I'd missed her.

I guess you never forget the dog you had in the years when you grow into a man. Your constant, unjudging companion. If you're happy, your dog is happy along with you. If you're sad, your dog sticks by you. If you do something stupid, your dog forgets it. If you do something good, your dog is always there to share it with you.

I looked into my dog's eyes and then she blurred as my tears came. I couldn't stop touching, petting, scratching her. After the initial freak out, she sat, fidgety, like she wanted to jump all over me, but controlled herself enough to keep butt to ground on the gravel shoulder of the road, her liquid, brown eyes staring up at me. Her tail wagged across the gravel, and her tongue lolled.

Though her fifteen-year-old master stood a few feet away, she stared at me with the unconditional love and loyalty that can only be shared by a dog and his best friend.

I'd forgotten the looks she gave me.

I swiped my hands across my cheeks, my eyes. Not trusting my face to be clear of tears, I needed to say something. I didn't look up from the dog, but I said, "You're thinking about the last time you saw your father, aren't you?" I watched his…my…eyes widen. "You're thinking why he didn't even recognize his own son."

"How did you...?" he said. I remember how confused I'd been in that moment.

I said, "Leo. I'm you."

15

"LEO. I'M YOU," he said. Then he smiled. His eyes were red. *Jesus, is he crying because he met Deena?*

"I know you don't believe me. But I know some things about you. And I know you can keep a secret if you need to, and this is one you will *need* to keep."

"Mister, I—"

"I'm not 'mister' to you. I'm *you*. Do you understand? I *am* you."

There's no way this guy was me. He was so *old*. I wouldn't be that old for like sixty or seventy years. But the way he stood. The way his voice got quieter when he stressed certain words like he did with *need* and *you* and *am*.

"How do you know I can keep a secret?"

"Because I know of three secrets you've kept up to now," he said. "Secrets you never told anyone. Not your mother, not even Jimmy."

I started a bit at him knowing the name of my best friend, met once mom and my stepfather married and I changed schools, but then again, he was an old guy. Old guys could find out anything.

I decided to call his bluff.

"Oh yeah? Tell me one, you're so smart."

"Okay." His eyes seemed to soften, almost like...

Like he was remembering...

"In grade three, Ms. O'Donoghue's class, who, by the way, you had a major crush on..." his voice trailed off as I felt the blush rising to my cheeks. "Huh," he said. "I guess I know of four secrets." He smiled, shook his head. "Anyway, in Ms. O'Donoghue's class, you were right into drag racing, and your two favourites were Don 'The Snake' Prudhomme and—"

"Tom 'The Mongoose' McEwen!" I said. "How did you know that?"

"I'm not done yet," he said. "In grade three, you had the Mongoose's Hot Wheels funny car and a friend—a one-time friend of yours—had the Snake's car."

"Brad," I said, not thinking.

"Right," he said. "Brad Steffen." He smiled. "Anyway, neither of you could keep your hands off those cars during school, so Ms. O'Donoghue took both cars and set them on her desk until the end of the day. The day ended with a test, and when you were done, you could head out to the school grounds until last bell." He stopped and shook his head. "Man, gotta love public school in the late Sixties."

"Why?"

"Kid, ask me when you're older." Then he laughed, but I didn't get the joke.

"Anyway, you finished before Brad, and O'Donoghue said you could get your car. She was at the front of the room and her desk was at the back. There were other kids finishing at around the same time, so there was a bit of confusion in the class." His voice got softer and he stared out at nothing. "You walked up to the desk and saw both cars there. The red Mongoose one that was yours, and that irresistible bright yellow Snake one that was Brad's. The Snake was your favourite, but the store had sold out when you had finally been able to drag your mom to get them. You'd wanted them both, but you'd really wanted the Snake's, because the Snake was your favourite."

I stared at him. He was reading my mind.

"So, you looked down at the desk. The cars were sitting on the back edge of the desk, the far side from where the teacher sat, right in front of you. There was couple of books to your right, a stack of mimeographed papers—God, I used to love the smell of freshly mimeographed paper—to your left, and a small vase with plastic flowers in it right in the middle." His hand slowly reached forward, palm down, fingers slightly curled. "You reached out your hand to grab the red car. You didn't stop, didn't look around, didn't even really think about it, you scooped both the cars up in your hand and—" here his hand snapped into a fist "—thinking you were so very smart, shifted the yellow one to your left hand and put it in your pocket as you held up the red one to O'Donoghue, raised your eyebrows and she gave you that smile that melted you and nodded okay."

"How do you—"

He'd been staring off at nothing, idly scratching Deena. "I'll tell you something else." Now he brought those scary-familiar eyes back around to my own. "You felt guilty for faking out O'Donoghue, but you never felt guilty for stealing that car from Brad. Even when he accused you of it."

And then I felt ashamed. He was right. He was right about the guilt. He was right about O'Donoghue's smile. Hell, he was right about the plastic flowers.

"But there were many times over the next three years when you wondered if all that bad luck, if all the bullying from that asshole was your penance for taking that car."

He's right about that too, I thought. *How the hell does he know all this?*

"You could have talked to O'Donoghue." I said. "You might have run into her, or looked her up."

He stood from where he'd been petting Deena. She didn't move, just shoved herself closer, pretty much sitting on his feet, staring up at him.

"That's pretty thin, but okay, you know what?" he said. "I'll give you that. Maybe I found a teacher from a few years ago and talked her up just to find out if you took something from her desk." He smiled. "I didn't, but I guess I could have." Smiling wider, he said,

"We always were good at coming up with the bullshit excuses, weren't we, Leo?"

He paced back and forth for a moment.

"Okay, then, here's the next one."

50

"OKAY, THEN, HERE'S the next one." I stopped pacing and faced him. I paused then, just for a quick moment because...my god, I was so damn young then. Fifteen. And I was so full of energy. I was immortal then.

And damn, but I'm skinny.

"When you lived in one of the apartments in the north end, a building pompously called *The Richelieu*, of all things, there was an evening when you were walking back from the skating rink. Again, gotta love the Seventies even more than the Sixties, because you were eleven years old, it was about 9:30, and you were alone." I looked off to the distance. "Wonder how often that happens these days?" I'm sure the younger me got lost at the "these days" comment, because I realized that, right now, on this gravel beside this highway, staring at my awkward, skinny, pimpled, fifteen-year-old self, we were still in the Seventies.

A strange, stray thought crossed my mind. The Seventies. Was *Star Wars* even out yet? Probably.

I rubbed a hand over my mouth, scrubbing at the close-cropped mustache and chin hair.

"Anyway. Not sure what got in my head then—maybe it was the week away and all the stuff that happened there, maybe it was Mom getting married in a few days, I don't know—but, walking through the parking lot for the building, there was car after car after car. Of course there was, right? I couldn't tell you when car antennas started being put in the windows instead of that silver, telescoping thing that grew out of the front or rear fender, but I do know at that point, tons of the cars in the lot had them. And somehow, it seemed like a good idea to grab one and bend it back and forth until it snapped off." I realized a little late that I referenced myself, instead of myself as him. *Goddamn, this is confusing.*

I turned my gaze back to him. *Me.* Me as a shockingly young boy. "And, instead of looking at that antenna in your hand—" *Your hand* this time. Not *my hand* "—and thinking, 'holy shit, I shouldn't do this,' it just spurred you to do it more. You walked around that damn lot and likely broke off ten or fifteen of the damn things."

I could read his face. He remembered this. Vividly.

Of course he did. I still remember it vividly. But the next day is even more vivid, isn't it?

"And I know you still have no idea why you did it...."

I knew he didn't.

"Because I *still* don't myself."

And I remembered this meeting from when I was him standing there. My mind had been roiling, as his was now, but even at fifteen, I had known I had to remain calm. He met my gaze, his eyes clear and bright behind glasses that, thanks to laser surgery, I no longer wore. I saw him hold his ground, not looking away, showing me he still didn't believe I was an older him. He was thinking, *If I look away, this strange old guy will think he's won, that he's convinced me.*

"And you didn't tell anyone," I said. "Instead, you hid those antennae—you called them 'antennas' back then—behind some bushes at the base of the apartment."

He continued to stare at me.

"But there's just a little bit more to that story, isn't there, Leo?" I smiled. And from the expression on his face, I remembered yet again exactly what I thought then. He was thinking, *no way. There's no way...*

15

NO WAY, I thought. *There's no way he can know all this.*

"Because two days later, Brad Steffen, our friend from Ms. O'Donoghue's class who eventually got the nickname Steffenwolf, our friend from the week at the camp, found you playing near the construction site for the next apartment they were building, the one that would eventually be called *The Summit Place*. And, at one point, after punching and kicking you, he held you over the hole they'd dug for the foundation of the building and threatened to throw you in."

I remember laying on the ground, my head and shoulders out over the hole, the only thing stopping me from slipping in headfirst was Brad's weight on my chest. I remember it being hard to hold my head up because he'd held me there so goddamn long. I remember my head tilting back, seeing the pit, upside down, then I'd pull up again, the muscles in my neck burning, my muscles so bunched and constricted it was hard to breathe. And Brad. Each time I pulled my head back up, Brad would swing a hand and slap my cheek. Hard. Then my head would fall back again and I would curse the tears that ran from my eyes.

"Shit on my sleeping bag, you fuck?"

I fucking hated Brad Steffen. We had been friends three years earlier. And since then, he'd been a bastard to me. Did I know why? Yeah, but hell, it was just a toy car.

"And, because, by then, he was almost a head taller and fifty pounds heavier—"

"I didn't fight back."

He seemed surprised, but then he smiled. "You didn't fight back." He paused. "Not right then."

"No." I could still see Brad's grinning face as he slapped me. I blinked back angry tears.

"No," he agreed. "Instead, you waited until the next day, telling no one. On the way to school, you passed by that pile of broken car antennas...antennae, found one that you could telescope down, and tucked it up the inside of your right sleeve."

I remembered the scratch I got from the sharp end where I had snapped it off.

"You had an unproductive day—then again, how productive is the last day of grade six, really?—spending most of your time hiding that damn antenna up your sleeve, making sure it didn't slip out. And staring at Brad."

And he never even noticed me, I thought. *He'd likely completely forgotten the day before. I was no more than a bug to him.* And, of course, it was the last day of school.

"Then," he said, "after school, you followed Brad, walking a safe distance behind him. Following him past your apartments to the nicer area just past that, to the houses where he lived. You hated him because he had everything and you had nothing and still he beat on you."

It was like this guy was actually in my head. *Maybe he is.*

"And then, when he walked up his driveway to the side entrance to his house, you dropped your books and, in possibly the smoothest motion you've ever done, you ran toward him while you dropped the antenna out into your palm and, grabbing it with your right, you telescoped it out to its full length with your left, then brought it up and swung it at him, hard."

My heart beat faster at the memory of speed and violence.

"The first shot caught him on his neck and cheek and he jumped back. But you didn't wait, because you knew if he got his feet under him you were dead, so you hit him again, the thin metal whicking out and catching him across the fingers."

He stopped here and stared at me, idly scratching Deena's head. He stared at me, but I could tell he didn't see me. His eyes were far away. Then he shook his head, coming back to himself.

"After that, it's a blur, but you can remember the high whooshing sound of the metal as it rose and fell, rose and fell, heard Brad's screaming and wondered if anyone would come, but amazingly, no one did. Maybe it was too early and everyone was at work, or maybe everyone knew what a bastard he was and that he was finally getting his due. Whatever the reason, no one came."

I remember worrying that his mom would come out. But she didn't.

"And when you were done, Brad was a mass of welts. He was crying and he was curled into a ball."

I remember all the welts, but I remember one vividly. It was on his left cheek, a vicious red line, ending in a dot of welling blood where the tip of the antenna had broken the skin. It looked like a lower case *i* had been written on his skin in red ink. I remember thinking, *the i stands for idiot.* He was pathetic.

"And you said—"

"'If you ever come near me again, I'll kill you.'"

"And he said—"

"'I'm sorry.'"

"And it wasn't enough."

"No."

"Because I fucking hated Brad Steffen."

"I fucking *hated* him."

"...Yeah."

"And it was the last day of school."

"Yeah."

"And I never saw him again."

"Yeah."

I think, *I see you through panes of glass and pains long past.*

I say, "You're really me, aren't you?"

"Yeah."

"You're me, but from the future."

"Yeah."

"How?"

"I don't know."

We stood, considering each other. I was struck by a few things. His weight. He wasn't fat, this future me, but he wasn't scrawny like I was. So skinny that, for years, whenever I had my shirt off, my hands inevitably crept up to hook over my shoulders, obscuring the map of bluish veins that traced under my skin, just below my collar bones.

His height. I was always tall for my age, and had learned to curl in my shoulders and hunch my head. I'd always hoped that if I didn't stick out from the crowd, the predators wouldn't notice me. It never worked. Instead, I was left bad postured and bullied. He stood, maybe a little round-shouldered, but taller and straighter than I ever have.

His face. I'd always seen my face as a blank slate. The term we'd learned in school was *tabula rasa.* I always saw something on other people's faces. Sadness, happiness, intelligence, cunning, suspicion, anger. My face didn't seem to carry anything like that, and maybe that was another reason for the bullying. They didn't see fear. They saw...nothing, and I think that angered them enough that they wanted to fill it with something more to their liking. Pain. Anger. Frustration.

And yet, on this man—this future-me—I saw the one thing I didn't expect.

I saw contentment.

That gave me hope.

Then the memories—memories of him, of seeing him previously—came back, and I realized that hope might be premature.

"It was you," I said. "It's been you every time, right?"

He looked at me.

"You've visited me before, haven't you?" I said.

50

"A COUPLE OF times," I said.

"A couple, yeah."

"Yeah. The first time you wouldn't remember. You were four and—"

"And you were standing by the road." I watched his face keenly. His eyes lost focus and he stared at the highway, not seeing anything. "It was night. I was in the backseat of the car and I woke up and looked out the window. I saw—"

"Me." I realized it was stupid to think he wouldn't remember that. I did. I always had.

"Holy shit."

"Yeah."

"And the second time was back at the cabin. After I..."

"After you shit all over a bunch of sleeping bags." I couldn't help it and didn't try. I laughed. So did he. Deena seemed to enjoy this. She got up and trotted between us, tongue lolling, tail wagging.

"Why do you keep showing up?"

"I don't know." Without either of us saying a word, he came closer, and we fell into step, walking down the shoulder of the highway.

"You've got no idea?"

"Well, maybe." He looked at me. "I don't even know what I should say to you, Leo. I don't know if there's rules around this. I don't know if I'm fucking something up in the future by just talking to you. I know you've read enough science fiction stuff to know what I'm talking about. So I'm not gonna say much, okay?" Still, I remembered exactly how much I'd given him. There really was no thought involved. I was mired in the biggest case of *déjà vu* anyone had likely ever experienced. This was *déjà vu*, but super-sized.

Déjà über vu.

He nodded. "Okay."

"So, here's my thought." I took a deep breath. "I think I showed up when you were four, because Mom and Dad split up right after." I glanced over. He was watching the ground, but he was listening. I knew because that's how I listened, with my head down. "Then I showed up at the cabin because you had no support."

"I didn't when Brad was holding me over a hole, either."

"I know. Maybe I didn't show then because it was just moments. Or maybe because you took care of it yourself."

"Maybe," he said, agreeing with me. Agreeing with himself.

"And I don't know what made the cabin different," I continued. "Maybe because it was an entire week of you floundering. I know it was one of the unhappiest times of your life."

"Yeah," he said, kicking at the gravel. "It was hell."

"And now, I'm here again."

"But nothing's bad now."

"Not now. No."

We walked, Deena trotting happily ahead, sticking her nose into tufts of long grass along the highway. I gave the younger me the time he needed.

Finally, slowing a bit, turning his head to me. "What's going to happen?"

"Your mom...our mom's...our stepdad...shit, this is weird." I took a second, got it straight in my head and just blurted it out there.

"After four years together, Mom and Bob's marriage is going to crash and burn in the next few days."

15

I KNEW BOB, my stepfather, could be an asshole. We basically hadn't talked much in the past couple of years. But he and Mom seemed tight. I stopped walking. My older self did too.

"What's going to happen?"

"I don't think I can tell you that, Leo."

"So..."

"So here's what I think I can tell you." He looked up at the sky, closed his eyes and took a deep breath. "God, I forgot how this place smells. The trees. The forest. The air."

I didn't say anything. I didn't really smell anything.

"It's going to get ugly, Leo," he said. "And it'll stay ugly for quite a while. You'll experience some things—" and here, I could see he was remembering stuff, because I saw his eyes water up. I hated that I cried too easily. Obviously that didn't change. "—you'll see some things and you'll be filled with more rage than you've ever had before."

I didn't know what to say. So I said nothing.

"You're going to think about killing him."

"Bob?"

"Yeah."

"Okay," I said. I couldn't see that happening.

"It's not even in your frame of reference now. But trust me, it's not because I'm putting the idea in your head. It's going to come to you from a different place. A really dark place."

"...Okay."

"And I'm telling you that you have to, for the first time in your life, you have to *not* fight back."

I flashed to Brad Steffen. The sound of the antenna as I whipped him.

"You're going to have to learn to stay calm."

"Why?"

"What do you mean?"

"Why do I have to stay calm?" I said. "If Bob becomes that much of an asshole..."

"Because Leo," and here he reached out and put his hands on my shoulders. It was the first time we'd touched. It felt electric. It felt like we were both buzzing, humming with an undefined energy. "He's going to say things to you, awful things to you. He's going to say something to you that will stick with you the rest of your life."

"Okay," I said. I wasn't getting it.

He sighed.

50

HE WASN'T GETTING it. I sighed.

Still, I couldn't tell him. I couldn't say that Bob, this supposedly loving father figure that, five years earlier, had gone through the pains of legally adopting me—well, adopting the then ten-year-old me—that just five short years later, Bob would look at me with a seething, burning hatred, his face twisted into someone I no longer recognized. And then he would say…

Jesus, I thought. *It still hurts to think about it.* Because I could see his face, almost smell the hate and disgust that twisted his face, that laced through his words.

His words. The hateful, awful thing he'd said to his fifteen-year-old son.

My stepfather's face—a man dead almost thirty years in my time—came back to me, those words, the ones that would haunt me for years, came out.

"I'm not going to get into detail, because, trust me, you're gonna live it soon enough." The thought crosses my mind that maybe I shouldn't even verbalize the phrase, because god knows I want to, if only to soften the blow.

I can still see the look on my stepfather's face. I can still hear the vitriol in his voice. I can still hear him as he says, "I've pissed on better than you, you worthless piece of shit."

He said that to me. He would say it to me.

He would put me lower than something he'd pissed on.

It hurt like hell when he said it. And all these years later, the hurt is just as sharp. Some pain doesn't pass.

"He's going to throw things at you, Leo," I said. "Things that he hopes will bring you down to his level." I dropped my hands from his bony, too-skinny shoulders. "I'm saying you can't let him define you with what he's going to say to you. You can't let him destroy you because of the hate and loathing he carries inside himself. He says what he says because of what *he* is, not what you are."

I looked into my own face, not yet scarred from the battles that would come so soon, and my heart broke for what he would soon experience.

"You have to remember one thing: That, no matter what he tells you, no matter what he calls you, no matter how worthless he makes you feel, you're better than that." I ducked my head, catching his eyes. "You hear me?"

"I hear you."

"Leo," I said. "The next few years are going to be filled with change. Some good, some bad." I couldn't help looking at Deena, remembering her fate. It had been bad. "But the biggest change you'll experience is that, soon, you'll no longer have to fight *against* others...

15

...INSTEAD, YOU'LL BE fighting *for* yourself."

He was still looking at me. I held his gaze, though it was hard for me. I wasn't used to looking people in the eye. *Fighting for myself,* I thought. *That would be a nice change.*

"You're going to go through some serious shit, Leo," he said. "But you'll get through it."

What could I say? He stood before me, telling me this. I had to believe him. He jigged his head in a way that felt very familiar. "Okay?"

"Okay," I said. Then a thought occurred to me. "Am I going to see you again?"

He tensed up a bit, then relaxed. "No."

"No?"

"Not that I can recall, anyway."

"Does that mean...?"

"I'm hoping we live a little longer than fifty," he said, a smirk curling the corner of his mouth.

"But we don't know, do we?"

"No," he said. "I guess we don't."

"But it gets better?"

Here, the smirk became a full-fledged smile. He handed me a worn piece of paper, a note of some sort. It had been folded so many times the paper almost separated at the seams. I unfolded it carefully. "I've been holding on to that note for thirty-five years, Leo," he said. "Back since, well, since I was the younger me in this conversation."

I read the note. It was my own handwriting. I little neater, but definitely mine. The note said,

Always remember: As bad as it gets, it gets better.

I folded it back up and tucked it in my back pocket. "You always seem to be passing me notes," I said, but I was smiling.

"I do, don't I?" He laughed then, and it was my laugh, and it was both weird and comforting.

"So, in answer to your question," he said, smiling warmly. "The answer is, yes. It gets better."

50

I LEFT HIM then, a smile on both our lips. I turned for a moment, one last sight of my dog. I saw her turn to me, her liquid brown eyes meeting mine. There was a slight wavering of the air, as though viewed through a heat haze, then I was back home. My home. In my time.

I stood, still smiling, looking down, remembering. Then I headed into the kitchen to pour the coffee from the pot I'd started before I'd left. It was just finishing. Five minutes had passed here. Maybe less.

I grabbed a big mug, put a spoonful of brown sugar in, filled a solid quarter of the mug with chocolate milk, then poured in the coffee and stirred. Looking outside, it was a beautiful evening, so I went to the patio doors and walked out to my back deck, enjoying the warm summer night.

Enjoying life.

Then he came around the corner of the house.

He seemed old. Older than me, though we were the same age. I knew this. It wasn't the stooped posture, the greying hair, the greyish flesh, the unshaven, sunken cheeks that betrayed him, though they all added to his apparent age.

No, it was that this man was obviously broken.

That broken quality, *that* was conveyed by all that he had become. I saw it in the narrowed squint of his eyes, partially closed like a dog waiting for a beating. I saw it in his shoulders, rounded and hunched against the weight of the world. I saw it in the curve of his spine and the angle of his eyebrows. I saw it in the set of his mouth.

I saw it in the way all of what he had become was directed toward me. *Aimed* at me.

And I knew...somehow I knew.

I had done this to him.

Then he started talking.

Though these were Brad Steffen's first words to me in four decades, it sounded like a conversation that had been running in his brain for a while. "Yeah, I lived in a nice place." He spit the words from his mouth like they had a foul, bitter taste. "Yeah, I had nice clothes. I had the nicest bike, the coolest things..." and here his voice trailed a bit. "...the coolest stuff..."

I struggled to keep up with his words as I moved toward him. He jerked. "You know *why* I had that great bike? Snake's Hot Wheels car? All that cool stuff? You wanna know *why* I had all that money all the time?"

"It's not important, Brad."

"No, man. It's not important to *you*, you piece of shit," he said. The hate steamed off him. "But it's fucking *every*thing to me."

"I'm sorry," I said. I kept my voice calm. "Tell me. Why did you have all that stuff?"

Tears sprang to his eyes, and the grim line of his mouth twisted. He actually gasped, caught himself, then shrieked, *"Because my fucking mother would beat the shit out of me!"*

"Ah shit, man, I didn't—"

He was past hearing. He stared at me, but I know he saw something else entirely. He cut off my words.

"Dad would come home...and do nothing. Fucking nothing, except to throw money at me." His hands twisted around each other, grabbing and clawing. "Shut up money. Quiet money." One hand pulled from the knot and grabbed at the bottom of his untucked shirt. "As if cash would fucking fix everything."

"Okay," I said. "All right." I still didn't know what this was. *Is he here as some part of a 12-step process? Or to kick the shit out of me?*

"So yeah, I went to school and acted all fucking cool. And yeah, I was an asshole to you."

"You were," I said.

"I know. I know I was," he said. "I don't know why I did it. It wasn't about that stupid fucking car. I could have gotten another the same day, and that was before she got bad with the beating. I don't know why I picked you."

And you don't know why your mom beat you, either, did you, Brad? I thought.

"But, after being beaten up by a girl—by my own fucking *mother*—then you come along." He swiped at the tears. "A skinny fucking little asshole. And you beat me too? Naw, it was too much. Too fucking much." He used the heel of his palms to clear the last of the tears. "I could be as big and tough as I wanted. It worked at school. I was tough there. But I couldn't fucking beat my mom."

"I'm sorry, man."

"Yeah," he said. "You're sorry. Fuck you, Oil. Would it have stopped you from whipping the shit out of me with a fucking car antenna if you knew?"

I could find no words that seemed right.

"Exactly."

He moved to a low bench on my patio. *Where the hell were all my neighbours?* I wondered. He sat.

"Dad fucked off a couple of years later. Left me there." He looked up at me. "Imagine that, huh? Fucking guy knows exactly what she was doing to me, left me there anyway."

I opened my mouth to say something. Nothing came out. "Took until I was almost thirty for that bitch to die. You know what she said to me?" He choked off a sob on the last word.

"No, Brad."

"She said…ah, she said, 'You're never gonna be tough enough, Bradley.' She said—" and he sobbed before he said it "—she said, 'I'm so ashamed of you'."

And I thought, *Jesus.* Because I knew exactly how he felt.

He paused a moment, staring down at my deck. "Her last fucking words to me were to criticize me. She couldn't beat me with her hands anymore, so she used her fucking mouth."

"I'm so sorry, man. I didn't know." I *was* sorry. I knew how those words could cut.

I've pissed on better than you, you worthless piece of shit.

"Yeah well, I think we've already established it wouldn't've made a fucking difference, would it?" His hands stayed in constant motion. Tugging at his jeans, running through his straggly hair.

"After you beat me with that antenna and left, I had another surprise visitor. Imagine. Me, eleven years old and the fucking belle of the ball.

"Anyway, this guy comes walking up my driveway. I thought it was some fucking pervert asshole, then he started talking. He didn't know what had happened to make him visit me, but he sure as hell remembered the place and time. He said he'd been pulled back."

He squinted up at me. "Sit down, Oil, because you're gonna think I'm ready for a padded fucking cell when I'm done telling you this next part." I sat, a sick feeling in my gut.

He pulled a pack of cigarettes from his shirt pocket, flipped the lid, pulled a cigarette out, pulled the lighter from the pack, cupped his hands. In all this time, I could have rushed him. Should have rushed him, but I needed to hear what he would say next.

He took a long drag on his cigarette, his long, greasy grey hair hanging between his eyes and mine. He squinted more from the smoke, then blew out the lungful.

"I went back in time and visited myself," he said.

I had been anticipating those words, but still, they caught me off guard. But I could also tell that he'd only done it the one time. And from the way he was acting—because Christ knew, this guy was a fidgeting nightmare—it had been recently. He was still in some sort of shock from it.

He'd accepted it as real, but it was still fucking his shit up.

"I went back and visited myself, eleven years old, half an hour from finishing grade six, still in my driveway, bleeding and hurting from your beating."

"When did you do this, Brad?"

"Don't fucking patronize me, Oil."

"I'm not."

"Whatever," he said. "Yesterday. Last night. Make you feel better?"

So his time difference is not the same as mine. Thirty-nine years instead of thirty-five. Weird.

"I should tell you something, Brad." I was trying to use his name. I'd heard that you made more of a connection if you used the person's name frequently.

"Yeah, well, fuck you," he said, seeming to disprove that theory. "It's my turn to talk." He took another long drag on the smoke, his eyes never leaving mine. "Anyway, we had a talk. Then I left him. I came back to right where I'd left from. The clock hadn't even turned over to the next minute yet, which, I gotta tell ya, fucked me up a bit."

I looked at the coffee cup still in my hand. I could empathize, but chose not to.

"Anyway, I got on the computer. Let me tell you, Google's a fucking wonderful thing. Can find anything on it." Another drag on the cigarette, then he used it as a pointer, stabbing it in my direction. "Including some asshole I hadn't seen in forty fucking years."

He reached behind him.

His hand came back with a knife in it. A long, well sharpened one.

Steffen regarded it for a moment. "My dad's. Besides mom, it was the only other thing he ever left me."

He stood, dropped his cigarette to my deck and ground it under a toe.

"The eleven-year-old me and…well…me, we talked, and from what I could piece together, all my shit seemed to fall apart after you stole that fucking car. By the time you shit on my sleeping bag, that was pretty much the commentary on my life. By the time you whipped me, my life was fucked." He toed the smashed remains of his cigarette.

"You don't understand, man. That week. That week away, it was heaven, Oil. I was away from my mother for an entire week. A week without her shit." He kicked away the remnants of the smoke. "Then you shit all over that too."

He chuckled humourlessly, then looked up at me. "And the stupid thing? I didn't even think to warn my younger self about dad fucking off, or having to wait so long for mom to die. It was so fucking far in my past and I was all fucked up being back in the early Seventies, staring at myself all beat to hell. Should have told little me to get the fuck out then and there."

He paused then, just for a moment. Then his eyes changed. There was a steely determination in his gaze.

"I don't know if there's a god, Oil, but I guess we're both gonna find out in a few minutes."

The realization of exactly why there had been no more visits between me and my younger self shot through my mind. I stiffened. I hoped to see my eighty-five-year-old self appear right now and set things right, but I knew damn well that wasn't going to happen.

I was going to die. Brad was going to kill me.

All this passed through my mind as he lunged forward and the knife arced.

I felt very little initially, just a sharp tug at my throat.

I closed my eyes.

All these years. All the time I'd held that piece of paper.

It gets better.

All these years. All these goddamn years I'd been lying to myself.

I opened my eyes and, after watching Steffen rip the blade across his own throat and fall out of my field of vision, I looked up.

I remembered the first time I'd gone back. Standing on that dark road, waiting to see myself in the back seat of that Pontiac. The sky had been dark and bejeweled with thousands of stars.

Stars that I could not see now, that I would never see again.

STORY NOTES

SO, THIS BIZARRE little story came from one of my oldest memories.

The scene where the child is in the car and he wakes up to see someone standing by the road near his house at night? I can only assume I dreamed this, however, roughly six decades later, the memory of this has never faded. I can feel the cold vinyl of the seats, see my father's face gently lit in the dashboard's glow, hear the low murmur of my parents' conversation. And yes, I can see that man standing there as the car goes by him.

It was clear enough that I remember the confused conversation the following morning with my mother, asking who the man was. She, of course, had no clue as to what I was talking about, but I was so convinced, I remember walking from the kitchen to the living room to look at the same spot, now hours later, half-expecting to still see him there.

The memory stuck with me, and I always wanted to write a story about it, but could never get a handle on what it'd be about.

Decades later, we ended up buying a house within walking distance of my old home, and I actually did take a walk there one lovely summer's day. When I got to the house, that is virtually unchanged externally, I simply stood—much like the man from my memory—facing the house, facing my memories.

An old guy came out from around the back of the house, and said, "Help ya?" And we ended up talking for most of the next hour, him showing me various things that I'd forgotten, or still remembered vividly. It was a good visit.

And on the way home, thinking about standing there, I thought, *what if it was me standing by that road that night, back around the time the Beatles were hitting Ed Sullivan for the first time?* Of course, I went into full what if?/why? mode and had much of the story parsed out by the time I got home.

Once again, I plundered much of my childhood to write this story, and every event, while obviously fictionalized, has a basis in reality.

So much of all this happened, including me ripping car antennas off of cars (though I was more like seven when I did it…and I still have no idea why I did). And I know you're wondering. Yes, a kid did hold my head over a pit in a construction site, and no I did not beat him, nor anyone else with an antenna. Or anything else.

I will also say that I really had no idea what to call this one until one day, while in the middle of writing it, I'd put on Billy Joel's second-best album, *Glass Houses* (his best is still *The Nylon Curtain*). There's a song on there called "Through The Long Night" that says something about all your past sins have since past…

…and just like that, I had my title. Seriously, how perfect is that?

So, pro tip for any writers out there, always be open, always have the radar up and running, inspiration comes from everywhere, when you least expect it. Always have the welcome mat out for it, and accept all callers.

Finally, yeah, I had to get in King's novel *CARRIE* because it truly was the story that shifted my mind over from simply enjoying stories to thinking I might actually be able to write them.

I'll leave that to you, reader, to decide how successfully I've managed that last part.

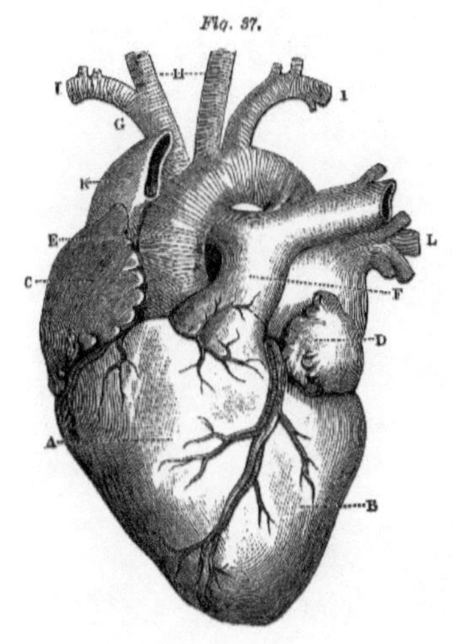

PART TWO:
ENEMIES & LOVERS

"People can be lovers and enemies at the same time, you know."

Willa Cather
My Mortal Enemy

DONE

JUST GIVE ME *the goddamn "I'm DONE!" Billy.*

As Billy huffed and puffed, Sarah ticked off the various ways she wanted Billy out of her vagina and out of her life.

Billy, for his part, existed only for the sex act, his body jackhammering into hers in a rhythm designed for his own maximum pleasure. Perfect hair over a perfect face. Billy enjoying the ride of his life. For her, it was simply a goodbye fuck, no more and no less.

He just doesn't know it yet.

ITS EARS PRICK up at the unusual noises, so unlike the night sounds in this area. A slight, mechanical screech of metal stressing against metal. It doesn't think much in language when it's in a state like this, but it gets a barely recalled image of springs and shocks.

Yes, it knows this. *A car.*

It remembers them.

Cars mean people.

There is another sound, fainter, muffled, of heavy, rhythmic breathing.

Sex.

Then it's on the move, ears twitching, sourcing out the sounds, and nose enticing secrets from the cool night air.

They will have fun together, the people and it.

They just don't know it yet.

♦♦♦

SARAH'S HEAD THUMPED against the back seat armrest, Billy's thrusts keeping time like a bass beat to a heavy metal song. She tried to reposition her left leg a little and settled for draping it over the back dash. Billy continued to pump, ignoring—or simply not noticing—her discomfort. He'd never been particularly adept at noticing much that didn't directly involve him.

Billy could take a long time to come, having long ago fallen into the delusion that this was as good for Sarah as it was for himself. But really, after all this time, with the lack of care he put into this so-called lovemaking, she wished he'd just blast through it like some of her girlfriends always complained their boyfriends did. *No, I had to pick a guy who's all stamina.* She envied her girlfriends' three-pump wonders right now. Not a lot of fun for her to have a guy who basically used her vagina to masturbate himself.

How the hell did I get here?

They'd been dating for over a year now, and she had always been a realist. Billy was a good-looking guy, and they looked good together, but even with that, she realized very quickly that arm candy simply wasn't enough. Not by a long shot. Oh sure, he had other points. He could be funny, some of his friends were nice…but overall, Billy missed the mark on more important things. And over the past few months, those missing important things had become more and more noticeable to Sarah.

She thought of her parents, married over two decades now and still happy. Sure, they squabbled and disagreed, sometimes they even fought. But mostly, they respected each other even though each still did things that irritated the other. Her father's damn coat, for one thing. An ugly navy-blue parka with an eye-wateringly repulsive orange lining and a matted fringe of fake fur around the rim of the hood. He'd owned the stupid thing so long that he had resorted to reinforcing the thinning elbows with duct tape. Small strips of tape also showed up haphazardly around the coat to repair the odd rip and tear. It was easily the most hideous thing Sarah had ever seen, and her mother hated it even more. But still, her father wore it every winter. He would pass over the stylish leather jackets or modern ski jackets her mother purchased in vain in favour of the hideous thing that had been outdated by the eighties.

And yet, for all of that, as much as she threatened to throw the thing out, somehow she never did. And Sarah knew why.

Because her mother respected her father.

That was something Sarah wanted for herself as well. The way Billy fucked her was just one symptom of his lack of respect. Sarah knew he'd finish, then go and have a smoke, leaving her alone. It's simply what he did.

And the sooner he does that, she thought, *the sooner I can get this over with.*

THE WOODED AREAS and the hills play tricks on its senses. It takes longer to pinpoint precisely where the sounds originate.

It took longer than it likely should have for it to remember to equate cars and roads. It crossed three before it makes the connection and begins following them instead of crossing them.

The additional time it spends searching only serves to build its anticipation of the sport to come from excitement to rage.

It wants to find them. *Now.*

But the small, human side of it that still held on in a corner of its brain makes it slow down. Sit and take a moment to both calm itself, somewhat, and to cast about for more sensory input.

And when it does, its nose immediately picks up the unmistakable musk of intercourse.

It stands, angles its ears this way and that, then lopes down the road. They are close. The sport would begin soon. They would be found.

The sooner it finds them, the sooner it will get this damnable hunger over with.

SHE VERY DELIBERATELY started working up to her spectacular, and completely manufactured orgasm, hoping that he would take that as a signal to let go.

God, seventeen and I'm already faking orgasms. She knew it was wrong, knew it sent the wrong signal—that Billy was the greatest lover in the world—but if she didn't, he'd half-heartedly pump at her for another half-hour before giving up. Then the ego-massaging questions would start.

It was bad enough that she was letting him get his dick stroked one last time. She wouldn't stroke his ego as well. *Well, aside from the bullshit orgasm.*

She built up to an enthusiastic but not too over-the-top crescendo, then slumped, her head still pounding against the damn armrest.

Billy worked up to his own, much more authentic release. She felt him tense a little more, felt his hands squeeze a little tighter. To be honest, this part wasn't bad, just as he approached his own finish. Though she knew it was completely reflexive, he held her a little tighter and she felt some passion from him, even if it was only a side effect of his own pleasure. It was for him, but she could, at least for a few precious moments, kid herself into believing it was for her instead.

Then his breaths changed to tight little Santa Claus noises—*ho! ho! ho!* – and he tilted his head back as though he would howl at the moon. She smiled, but kept it to herself. A small smile, because even after most of a year, she still could never predict when it would happen. She always tried to gauge from his twitching body and huffing, but whenever she figured it couldn't go on, it did.

Then finally, he threw his head back even more, his Adam's apple jutting prominently from his taut neck muscles. He stopped the huffs, holding his breath, pushing himself as deep as he could into her, gathering his strength, then, in a rush of air, yelled, *"I'm DUUUUNNNN!!"* and came in great bucking waves before dropping heavily down on her, his breath irritating in her ear, ruffling her hair. She could barely breathe.

His breathing slowed to normal as Sarah continued to take shallow breaths, doing her best to not push him off her. Finally, he lifted himself up and pulled out.

"Gotta take a piss, babe," he said. "Probably grab a smoke while I'm out there." She pulled her legs up to give him room to slip his feet into his crumpled jeans and pull his underwear and pants back up. She felt what he'd left behind leaking coldly out of her.

He opened the door, letting the brisk October air in. She saw he'd left his pants low enough for his ass to show whitely above the waistband, like he was one of those idiot low-riders that showed way too much underwear. For him though, she knew this was simply for expediency. No sense in doing the pants up only to undo them again for a piss.

He held the door open, letting even more cold air in. "While I'm out here, you wanna fold up the blanket before anything soaks through?" Sarah restrained herself from mouthing the next words along with him. "The old man'll kick my ass if anything stains his seats." It was the usual spiel and the cleanup was always left to her.

He closed the door and she sat up, the leather cold against her bare skin. She could see his blurred form through the fogged rear window and felt the small jolt as he leaned against the side of the car to take his piss.

She gathered up some of the ratty beach towel and wiped herself as clean as she could, then pulled her own jeans up as well. She folded the towel up to keep the wet deep inside and tossed it on the floor in the front where he wouldn't miss it.

Then, she sat and waited. She knew he'd be a while. He'd pee. He'd smoke. He'd fix his hair. He'd look at the goddamn stars. He'd make her wait.

She glanced out the rear window again and saw his outline, dim in the moonlight, a small red glare of a cigarette.

She turned back around and looked out the side window closest to her. The window was still fogged, so she brought a finger up and drew a circle. Two dots for eyes. A downturned line. Not a happy face.

That was her right now. Not happy.

ITS TASK BECOMES easier as it gets closer. The sounds are more pronounced. The smells sharper.

Then there comes, just back from the road, the slight mechanical sound of a vehicle door opening, and someone speaking. It hears the words, but in its present state, it cannot understand them.

However, the story is very clear. The fug of sex drifting from the man's penis, then the sharper, acrid odour as he urinates. The patter of the liquid hitting the dirt. The sigh of release.

Then, more sounds, fumbling, before a flare of flame, and the point of red, a beacon for it to follow, as if the stink of the thing in the man's mouth isn't enough.

It treads more carefully now, predator stalking prey, but there's a lightness in its step.

This is what it is. Happy.

SHE'D ASKED BILLY—still called William Stradlater Junior if his mother happened to be particularly pissed at him—if they could get together tonight to talk. She stressed the words *to talk*, but they seemed to whistle right by his perfect hair. "You lookin' for a little action?" he had asked, an expectant gleam in his eye.

"Billy," she'd said. "I'd like to *talk*." She was damn near tempted to bust out the *William Stradlater Junior* tag herself at that point.

"Okay, babe," he said, placating. "Okay. We can talk." A salacious grin twisted his lips.

Sarah had talked to her mother about Billy, about how he just didn't seem to be the one. Her mother had suggested she may be outgrowing him. She'd smiled when she told Sarah that women always mature faster than men. Smiled wider when she said some men don't ever mature at all.

Then she'd put her hand on Sarah's, resting it lightly over her daughter's. "You do what your heart tells you to do," she said. And Sarah had known what that was. Had, in fact, known it for months.

Her mother had just underlined it for her. So, she'd asked Billy to talk.

She'd had to talk him out of inviting friends. She'd had to make it clear she wanted to be alone with him. Of course, Billy being Billy, he'd read the signals all wrong.

He'd picked her up that night in his father's car. When she hopped in, he'd asked her where she'd wanted to go. She didn't have a destination in mind, and made a critical error in saying she didn't really care, instead of suggesting a fast-food place or a coffee shop. It wasn't until she realized he'd pointed the car toward the more rural area north of the city that she began to expect what Billy had in mind.

"Billy," she'd said to remind him. "I said I wanted to *talk*."

She watched that same small grin—a grin she'd first loved, then learned to despise—slide across his lips again as he drove, wrists loose on the wheel. "I know, babe. We'll talk. Promise." He kept the car pointed north. He took one hand off the wheel and placed it on her knee. "It's just that Little Billy needs some lovin', y'know?" His hand crept up her thigh. "Then we can have that little talk, okay?"

She stopped his hand's roving path mid-way. "Little Billy isn't getting a damn thing while Big Billy's driving."

That was enough for Billy to find a secluded spot, an old driveway that now led to nothing but a dense copse of trees. He drove through the trees, then past them to the other side. "So we can still see the stars," he'd said. She knew he'd had no intention of looking at the stars until after he'd gotten his dick wet and then had a cigarette. That was just how Billy rolled.

So now, here she sat. Billy had, as usual, gotten what he wanted while she still waited for the real purpose of the night to start.

When he finally got back in the car, she was going to tell Billy she didn't want to see him anymore.

She didn't expect him to take it well, but she also didn't think he'd be overly disappointed either. She'd seen the way he looked at some of the other girls in the school. With more than just a passing interest.

Then again, if she was honest with herself, she had to admit she was doing the same damn thing.

Lately, she'd been focusing her attention on one specific boy. He was the exact opposite of Billy. Nothing to really look at, but still there was something about him. A vulnerability. An openness.

And he'd caught her looking too.

Sarah wasn't the type to screw around on her boyfriend, no matter how much of a dick he was. Better to break it off clean and start fresh. That was what she wanted to accomplish tonight. A clean break from Billy.

Jesus Christ! What's taking him so damn long?

It was time to get this over with.

♦♦♦

IT WATCHES THE prey as the red light at his mouth flares and dims, flares and dims. It will not approach while the man has the thing.

It can't remember what it's called, but it knows that thing is as hot as it is bright.

The man takes forever with the glowing thing.

Then, just at the point where it is about to go against its own judgment, it sees the man throw the glowing thing at his feet, hears the sizzle as it lands in the acrid pool of urine and extinguishes.

The man exhales a last, pungent breath of smoke, and then it is on the move.

It is time to get this over with.

♦♦♦

JUST AS SHE turned to look out the rear window again, the car rocked. It was likely Billy pushing hard against it, screwing around, but also letting her know he was done and they could have "that little talk" now.

Instead, the car rocked again. And she heard something. A squealing scrape, as though a screwdriver had been drawn down the side of the car. The car rocked again. Then again.

Then she heard Billy scream.

Goddamn him! she thought. *This is* so *not the time to be screwing around!*

"Billy!" she yelled. She pushed the seat forward to scramble into the front.

The car rocked again. A thunderous boom as something hit the car. Hard.

She wormed to the driver's seat and started the car to lower the fogged window. No way she was opening the damn door. The window cracked and she caught a glimpse of two glowing, yellow eyes. She pawed at the controls to get the window back up again.

Hyperventilating now. Something jumped on the hood of the car. Two legs. Dark. "Jesus!" she yelled.

Then the front window spiderwebbed as something hit it dead centre. The safety glass held, but the window bent inward. Another thunderous boom, this time on the roof. And another. The roof of the car pushed downward, bowing into the interior.

A high, keening whine. Sarah realized it was her. The roof boomed again, then again.

The front window, again.

Then the car jumped as the weight left it and Sarah caught movement out of the corner of her eye. Whatever was out there was back at the side window again. The window shattered, pebbles of glass showering her as she screamed. She spit them out as she frantically grabbed for the shift lever to put the damn car in drive.

She pulled at it, pushed at it, yanked on it, but it wouldn't fucking move.

Something splashed her. It was the taste, not the sight of the blood that woke her up. Her left side gleamed wetly, almost black in the cold October moonlight.

Billy?

She realized then that she needed to push the brake to get the car into gear. She slammed her foot down on the pedal as something shot through the window and raked her scalp from the back of her head to the front. She heard a wet ripping sound as flesh—her flesh!—pulled away from bone.

Tendons shrieked as her jaw flexed, her mouth opening as wide as it possibly could as she screamed, expunging every bit of the air in her lungs. Tears streamed down her face as she finally got the goddamn gear shift into drive. She lifted her foot and slammed it back down, a little to the right, pounding the gas pedal to the floor, doing everything she could to push it into the ground, her butt rising from the seat with the effort. The car jumped forward. The sound of the screaming engine and the thump of gravel and clumps of sod pounding at the rear wheel wells filled the car as the tires fought for purchase. Then the vile thing came back in the window again. This time in front of her face, reaching for one of her arms. She batted at it with a hand, pulling away from the feeling of—

Of what?

Hair?

Fur?

A bear. Goddamn bear attacked us.

Whatever it was, it grabbed the wheel and wrapped a meaty fist around it.

A fist. *Not a bear.*

She risked a look to her left, saw a sloping head that came down to a snout and thought bear, then dog, then gave up. It snarled back at her. The car careened back down the road Billy had driven them up just an hour earlier.

They approached the copse of trees again and Sarah wondered desperately how the thing held on. She looked again, saw the snarl again, saw the rhythmic rising and falling of that head, realized the thing was running—*It's fucking running*—beside her.

She did the only thing she could do. She cranked the wheel to the left to push the thing off balance. Its hand fell from the steering wheel, grabbed madly for her face, her arm, anything. It caught the rear-view mirror and tore it off and it was gone, no longer beside her.

The car hit a tree and Sarah saw the shattered window fly at her, realizing only at the point of impact that it had actually been her flying at the window.

SHE WASN'T OUT long. But when she came to, she came back to instant panic. The thing now squatted on the hood and reached for her through the shattered ruins of the front window. She couldn't fight it off and it pulled her out like an infant from a car seat.

It held her, half in, half out, of the damaged vehicle and stared at her. She saw with some small measure of satisfaction that she had injured it. It bled from a wound on the side of its head and a deep gash on one arm.

Got you too, fucker.

It stared at her. Blood streamed into her eyes and she did what she could to blink it away. It pulled her forward and she caught its sharp, fetid odour as it opened its mouth to lick at the blood, its tongue long and moist and hot.

You're a dog? No, wolf. But, with hands?

The werewolf reared back, opened its jaws, then shot forward and she felt the jaws contract on her face. A brief shock of pain.

Then Sarah had one last thought. *I'm done.*

IT FEEDS WELL this night.

It takes the man first however, the woman in the car is definitely the one it enjoys more. That one obviously didn't suck on the glowing things.

It takes its time, enjoying the sharp smell of blood and brain fluids, the moist sounds of the guts as it scoops and nuzzles them into its jaws. The cracking sound of the bones and the smell and taste of the marrow is shockingly pleasurable.

The bright moon above, its constant companion, looks on quietly until it has taken everything it wants.

And the moon watches as it finally rises, its tongue swiping away the last flecks of blood and offal, to find a place to hide and sleep.

It's been a productive night.
But now, it's done.

STORY NOTES

ANOTHER ONE THAT might sound familiar, if you've read my *Aphotic* series. This is the lightly re-written opening to the third book in the series, *BLOOD LOSS.*

Again, I had no intention of parceling out a portion of my novel as a short story, however, I saw a submission call for a werewolf anthology, so I gave it a shot.

Apparently they were unimpressed, as I got a fairly quick form rejection, as I recall.

No matter, I got something out of it anyway.

Originally, the opening to the novel that I lanced out to its own short story only had one point of view, and that was Sarah's. All that in-between stuff from the wolf's point of view? Yeah, it didn't exist.

And, the single point of view works quite well as the opening to a novel, however, for the short story, I needed to bring some tension, some danger in sooner, to hook the reader. So, what better way to do that than to let the reader know there's something stalking Sarah and Billy?

I ended up liking that point of view enough that I transplanted it back to the opening of the novel.

I also used to really enjoy driving the quiet roads north of the city I was born and raised in. Back then we referred to them as "the

Concessions" because it was "Concession Road 1" and "Concession Road 8" and so on. Those placeholder names are rapidly disappearing these days as more and more houses are built and more big box stores fill that once-quiet farmland.

But, back in the early 80s, driving those quiet roads in the middle of the night, there was something magical about them. However, if you stopped somewhere—maybe to have a piss, or a smoke—the feeling could take a turn from magic to malevolent very quickly. I've felt it. Standing beside my car on a dirt road that just leads to more dirt roads and farm fields...anything could be out here in the middle of the night. Under a full moon.

I remember thinking that on one of those drives. That was the seed for this story.

One final note...in this story, Billy's orgasmic catchphrase is, obviously, "I'm done!" However, in the original novel opening, it's actually "Geronimo!" Why?

Because I remember spending a night with a bunch of fast food coworkers way back in the early 80s and the conversation, as the night wore on, flitted from topic to topic, but the only one I now remember is the coworker who was so sick and tired of her boyfriend yelling "Geronimo!" loudly in her ear as he released.

I thought that was the funniest damn thing, and I remember thinking right then and there that I had to file that away for use somewhere down the line.

Always be careful what you say in front of a writer. If it's weird enough or interesting enough, I guarantee you it's gonna show up somewhere on the page.

THE LAST TREE IN THE GARDEN

NOW

TESS WILLIAMSON SITS in one of the two chairs in the shade of the old red maple, cradling a cup of coffee in her worn, calloused, but still supple hands. The other chair is empty and, staring at it as long as she can, wishing as hard as she can, she cannot relieve that chair of its heartbreaking emptiness.

It is the same emptiness that has hollowed out her soul.

Blinking away fresh tears—she'd cried more of the damnable things in the past twelve hours than she had in all of her eighty-one years—she pulls her blurring gaze from the chair's emptiness and looks up through the leaves of the tree.

It's a thing of beauty, this tree, and she and Graham had spent many mornings under it, sometimes chatting amiably, but often just quiet, smiling at the chittering of the chipmunks and the singing of the birds. Looking up now, she easily finds the nest high in the boughs, lit through a reddish filter of the sun on the leaves. Here and there, small spots of perfect blue, the sky peeks through.

Graham had loved this tree. Each year, he watched, fascinated, as a nest was built, and new families were born. There had been a lot of life that had come from this tree, the first one that Tess and Graham had planted under all those years ago, starting in, appropriately enough, 1969. The Summer of Love. The only tree they hadn't actually planted. The first one standing in what had been a barren field more than five decades ago.

Swiping at the moisture on her cheeks, Tess turns to look out over the land that runs behind their house. The first time they had come here, it had been just a grassy field, flat as far as the property extended, ending with a shallow pond before rising into small hills.

Now, the area is filled with trees. Each one a marker of an important event in their lives.

Tess and Graham had never called it a forest. The term had always seemed a bit too audacious for what they had started. "Never want to lose sight of the trees for the forest," Graham had once said, that lovely lopsided smile of his, brightening his face. Maybe someday, long after they were both gone, it might become a forest, but for now, they—or rather, just Tess now—call it a garden.

Their garden of memories.

Tess reaches out a hand to the gnarled rough bark of the maple, lightly exploring it. *It all started with this one,* she thinks, and she looks back up through the leaves to the blue sky beyond—a perfect day—and thinks again that this perfect tree on this perfect day symbolized their perfect life. Her's and Graham's perfect life.

This was the start of it all. Starting all the way back in '69.

All because of Cynthia.

Thank God for Cynthia, Tess thinks.

1969

TESS CROSSED THE concrete floor of her apartment's underground parking garage, the heels of her go-go boots clacking as she walked, the harsh noises echoing through the structure. Her mind whirled chaotically with what she had to do today, as her fingers clenched in a fist, three keys jutting from between her fingers, just like her father had taught her nine years earlier when she'd passed her driving test. *There's a lotta creeps out there, baby girl,* he'd said. *Y'gotta be ready for them.*

Three years after that, he was dead and buried beside Tess's mother. At nineteen, she'd had to grow up fast.

She reached her car, a rusted out '64 AMC Rambler Classic. It didn't look pretty, but it ran, and it had a good 8-track player, so she loved it.

She unclenched her fist to get to the Rambler's key to unlock the door, and promptly dropped them. The jingling crash reverberated off concrete walls in a way that made Tess happy.

Until she noticed the flat tire.

"Crap." She remained there a second, just looking at the tire, the rim nestled in a flaccid, rubbery cradle. *Dammit,* she thought. *Now I'm gonna get filthy changing the stupid thing, and have to go back up and clean up before Cynthia's.* Dad had taught her how to change a tire, too. *Y'gotta know some basic maintenance,* her dad had said. *Whaddya gonna do if y'getta flat in the middle'a nowheres?* However, Dad had never had to change a tire in a miniskirt.

Still pissed at her luck, she was distracted as she straightened, so she wasn't ready when she saw the reflection in the Rambler's side window, coming at her quickly, silently. Before she could react, someone had one strong hand over her mouth, tight to her nose, and had cranked her head back so she was left blinking and staring at the concrete ceiling with its pipes and moist areas and caged light bulbs. Then she felt the sharp pressure against her exposed throat. A knife.

"No noise or I do it now. Right now," he said, his breath hot in her ear, the smell of his fingers—*Ivory soap?* –in her nose. "Get me?" he said. She nodded, slowly and carefully, making sure that knife didn't press any harder against her neck.

"Gimme your keys," he said. He held her tight to him, her ass tight against his crotch. He was hard.

You find yerself in some shit, her dad had said, *y'just go along as best y'can. Do what they want, til y'can kick 'em in the nuts, er poke 'em in th'eyes, y'hear?* She'd wait for her chance. For now, she raised her hand and gave him the keys.

"Around back of the car," he said, and tightening his grip on her mouth, he pulled her around the car so they were between the back bumper and the wall of the garage. "Gonna let go of your mouth now, okay? You gonna scream? Go nuts?"

She slowly shook her head.

"Good girl." He dropped the knife so the tip poked against her belly, only the thin polyester material between blade and flesh, then he carefully released his grip on her mouth. The smell of Ivory soap lingered, as she licked her lips. He stepped around in front of her, knife still poised. He looked…familiar.

Tess knew this was where she should start begging him to spare her, to not hurt her, to not kill her, that he could leave now and she'd tell no one.

But seeing the look on his face, she knew she'd be wasting her time.

"What do you want?" she said, her voice remarkably calm.

"I saw you last night," he said. "You and that girl at the bar."

"Me and—"

"Cynthia," he said. "Yes." And that yes had layers, worlds of meaning hidden in it.

Then she knew. "You were that guy."

He smiled.

"That guy last night," Tess said. "You sent over two drinks for us."

He nodded. "The guy that you accepted the drinks from, and didn't even acknowledge."

"No," Tess said. "It's not like th—"

"It's exactly like that," he said, the spit sparkling her face. She ignored it.

"No," she said, keeping her voice calm, calm. "I wanted to go over and at least thank you. I did. But—"

"But you didn't," he said.

"You're right, we didn't. Let me finish." She paused a moment, waiting to see if he really would. A small nod, more a quick jerk of his head. *Okay, at least he's listening.*

"We didn't because of Cynthia." The next part was a gamble, but she figured, play the honesty card, and go all in. "She thought you looked creepy. Letmefinish," she tossed out, because she saw him open his mouth to speak. He closed it again.

"Thank you," she said. Closed her eyes. Took a breath. "Okay, she thought you looked creepy. I actually thought you were kind of cute." He rolled his eyes. "Hey, believe what you want. You're gonna kill me anyway, so what the hell have I got to gain from bullshitting you, right?"

He smiled. Actually freaking smiled at her.

"Can I at least know your name?"

He considered for a moment. "Graham."

"Graham?"

"Yes," he said sourly. "Like, 'discoloured pork.' Gray. Ham. Graham."

She actually laughed at that. "Discoloured pork. I like that, Graham. That's funny." He didn't look like he was buying, so she went on. "See, that's exactly what I said to Cyn last night. I told her I thought you were kinda cute and said you looked like you might have a sense of humour. She said she didn't give a shit, and I threw back what my mom used to say. She always said, 'Never marry for looks, baby girl, cuz looks'll fade, but a sense of humour, a guy that can make you laugh? That's forever, sweetie.' And I believe her."

"And I just made you laugh."

"You did." She smiled again. *Why am I smiling? He's going to kill me.* Still, he had made her laugh. "So, hey, that's forever," she finished. Lamely, as far as she was concerned.

They were both silent for a few moments. Graham studied her. Taking his time. The silence stretched. And Tess didn't feel any awkwardness. She didn't mind his eyes on her. She thought about that hardness that had been pressed up against her, as well. She didn't mind that either.

"So why didn't you come over yourself?"

"Because," she said, and allowed all the frustration she could muster creep in to her tone, "I waited until Cyn had to pee—it never takes long, I swear that girl has the bladder of a gerbil—and I was gonna come over and talk to you. But by the time she got up—"

"I was gone."

She let out her breath. "You were gone."

"And then?"

"And then, I was pissed. Seriously. I probably had a shot with you, right?"

He didn't give her anything, but there was…something…in his eyes.

"Anyway, nothing much was happening, so we called it a night. I drove her home, dropped her off. Thought about—and again, I ain't shitting you—going back to the bar to see if I could find you, but decided against it. You'd left. I came home instead."

"Which brings us to now."

"Almost."

"Almost?"

"Well, yeah. You caught me heading out."

"You were going to meet up with Cynthia again."

Tess studied him, narrowing her eyes. "Yes," she said, drawing the word out.

"Maybe catch a movie. Maybe *Easy Rider*."

"Yeah, how did you—"

"Cynthia wanted *The Wild Bunch*, but you're more a Peter Fonda type than a William Holden girl."

Then she was clueing in. "You've talked to Cynthia."

"Oh, my dear Theresa—"

"Tess," she said. "I despise Theresa."

"Fair enough. I've done much more than talk to Cynthia, though we did have a long, fruitful chat."

"What did you do?"

"Don't ask questions you don't really want the answer to, Tess."

"What. Did you. Do?"

He studied her, as though judging whether she truly did want the answers. "Since you asked so nicely," he said, then sighed. "There's no easy way to say this, so…I fucked her, then I killed her."

"You killed her."

He smiled. "I did."

She was quiet for a long time. *Honesty card,* she thought. *All in.*

"Then I guess you did me a favour," she said.

His smile dimmed, then went strange. Strained. He cocked his head to the side slightly, reminding of a dog. "How so?"

She lifted a hand, indicating the trunk of her car. "May I?"

He put some pressure on the knife in her belly. "As much as I believe I may be making a stupid mistake, I must admit you've intrigued me, Tess. Just remember I can open your organs to the world in a heartbeat."

And oh, why did that phrase catch in her mind? *Open your organs to the world.* She felt that. Deeply. Arousingly.

Still, she held it close and only responded with, "I understand."

"Move slowly."

"You have my keys." He selected the correct one and slid it into the lock of the trunk. A twist of the wrist and the back of the car was unlocked. She approached it, moving slowly, and said, "I'm just going to open this, okay? Then I'm gonna just step back."

"No tricks."

"No tricks."

"Go ahead."

She opened the door and stepped back as promised. Graham looked at her. She indicated the contents in the back of the car.

He glanced quickly, then studied it more closely. "What is this?"

"Rope. A tarp. A saw. And a home-made garrote, made from some piano wire and two wooden dowels. I'm kinda proud of that, actually."

He looked at her.

"Isn't it obvious, Graham?" It was her turn to smile. "I was going over to her place to kill that stupid bitch myself."

NOW

SITTING IN HER chair, the coffee cooling in the mug, she remembers Graham back then, fifty-odd years ago. Her hand moves to her throat, to where the blade had pressed against it. She still feels it, the potential behind its weight, the promise it held.

And Graham. Back then, he had been all potential, all promise. The smell of him. The feel of him. Lord God Almighty, he had been exciting.

Five decades on, Tess can still hear the faint echoey sounds of that parking garage, the building long since torn down for more expensive condos in the Eighties, and she can still smell that damp concrete smell, and his smell, Graham's Ivory soap smell. She closes her eyes and breathes in, filling her lungs with the memory of him.

It was obvious as he stood, staring at her murder kit, that there had been an attraction between them. She'd felt it as he held that blade to her neck. That hardness, tight up against her ass. Hell, she'd felt it the night before, though it had been more dormant, more promise than feeling, when she'd first seen him.

It was in the confidence of his face, in the way he bore himself, in his grin. But it was also in the sure way he talked.

But there was a deeper attraction to him, one that announced itself the first time she felt that knife edge on her throat. Graham had been someone who existed so far outside society's boundaries he was almost in a different world. For him, it wasn't even that he was ignoring the rules, it was as though the rules simply didn't apply to him.

As though he had his own rulebook, separate and distinct from the rest of society's.

And to Tess, that made him a bit godlike to her.

She'd come to learn to love not only his meticulousness, but also his almost desperate need for spontaneity.

But, she knows, she also brought much to the table as well. She knows Graham had, at first, taken advantage of her clumsiness, and later, somehow become enamoured with her clumsy, messy way of approaching life, even as her "slobbishness" as he called it, drove him bonkers.

But most importantly, she *got* him. She understood Graham.

Because deep down, though they were very much opposites, they were also cut from the same cloth.

1969

GRAHAM DUG THROUGH the items and gradually, gradually, Tess felt him let his guard down. Not a lot, but enough that she could breathe again.

"You're really not shitting me, are you?"

"No."

He stood straight, staring into the car, the knife now hanging, seemingly forgotten, in his hand. She could very likely be able to, if not grab it, at least slap it out of his hand and make a break for it.

But somehow, she felt this was the exact wrong move.

Instead, she gave him the time he needed to process and, instead, studied him.

He was a little taller than her, maybe four inches or so. Tess was a tall girl, what Cynthia called "statuesque" but that descriptor felt vaguely insulting as it fell from her lips. So that would put Graham over six feet, but not by much.

His hair was longish, over his collar, but not what would be considered hippie-long. And it was clean. He was clean. The vogue lately for her age group and their antiestablishment ways was to eschew anything valued by *the Man*, though Tess had never really fully understood who, exactly, *the Man* was. But part of that was a distressing habit of not bathing, which she really wasn't into.

Obviously, Graham wasn't either. He actually smelled good.

And, while not classically handsome, he was a good-looking man, his deep chocolate eyes a little sad, but a mouth that seemed to naturally curl to a smile to offset those eyes. Though he didn't look anything like the man, Tess thought his looks ran more to Bogart than Gable. Not a stunner, but not someone she'd necessarily kick out of her bed.

Why am I thinking about him in my b–

He stepped back from the Rambler's door. "Let's go for a ride," he said.

"Where are you—"

"I'm not taking you somewhere to hurt or kill you, if that's what you're asking," he said. "Quite the opposite, actually."

She hesitated. He raised the knife and she thought, *here it comes.*

He tossed the knife up lightly, making it spin in the air just above his hand, and he caught it just as lightly by the blade, the handle toward Tess. "Take it."

This time, she didn't hesitate. She didn't lunge for it either, simply reached out and took hold of the handle. He released his hold on the blade. "I want you to trust me," he said. "You hold on to it."

He's crazy, she thought. *I could kill him right now and no court in the land would convict me.* Then she thought, *And he knows it. That's why he knows I'll trust him.*

She made her decision. "Okay," she said, and tossed the blade in the trunk of the Rambler and closed it. "Your car or mine?"

1969

GRAHAM CHANGED HER tire. They took her car.

When she asked where they were going, his answer didn't surprise her in the least. And fifteen minutes later, they arrived at Cynthia's basement apartment. As Tess slowed to park, Graham said, "Keep driving. Go around the corner to find a place to park." He gave her that easy smile. "Trust me, you won't want anyone witnessing your car there today."

She parked two blocks away, and they walked back toward the house.

They walked casually to the side of the house and entered through Cynthia's entrance. Graham produced a key and unlocked her door, and they were inside.

The smell was the first thing to hit Tess. A heavy odour of copper, and an undertone of piss and shit.

"Sorry for the smell," he said. "Unfortunately, it kind of can't be helped."

Tess tried pulling her blouse up to her nose, but it left too much of her midriff uncovered for her liking. Instead, she made the conscious decision to just deal with it. Graham seemed to take notice of this. He gave her a short nod and a quick smile. "You ready for this?"

She gave a short nod of her own, not trusting her voice just now.

Graham led her to the door to Cynthia's bedroom.

It was an abattoir.

Tess was speechless.

Her bedroom, with its greenish shag carpeting normally the only colour offsetting the white walls and white furniture, was now awash in a deep red, almost purple, of the blood that, twelve hours before, had still run through Cynthia's veins.

"Did you just kill her?"

"What do you mean?" Graham asked. "She's been dead for—"

"Did you just kill her, or did you…"

"Did I fuck her first?"

"…yes."

"I fucked her first, Tess."

"Yes. Right," she said, with an irritated shake of her head. "You told me that. Back at the car." Tess remained standing at the threshold, her feet inches from the bloodstains. She let her eyes travel around the room, taking in the furniture, the small desk where Cynthia would try and make herself up and usually fail. The desk was usually a mess of makeup and powders. Now, it was coated with a splash of red. She glanced to the *2001: A Space Odyssey* movie poster, banks of computer lights arcing across Keir Dullea's space helmet. It was a movie that had fascinated the hell out of Cynthia, where Tess had simply found it impenetrable and confusing as hell. Graham had added a splash of blood to the helmet.

Then she turned to Cynthia herself.

Cynthia lay face up, her dead eyes staring blankly at the ceiling, her lips slightly parted, as though she was about to say something.

Tess stared at her eyes. Her mouth. Her breasts. Her pubic hair arcing down between her spread legs.

In a whisper, she said, "Tell me."

When Graham remained silent, she turned to him, met his eyes. "Tell me," she said again. "Tell me everything."

1969

HE TOLD HER everything. He stood behind her and, at some point, as her eyes continued their slow crawl around the room, he put his hands on her hips. But he kept talking. He spared no detail.

It took him almost an hour to tell her everything.

And as he did, in that hour, Tess realized that more than just Cynthia had passed from this world. Everything Tess knew, everything she had valued, everything she had considered important…all of it passed away as well.

As Graham spoke, she felt his words first opening her up, punching holes in the framework of her reality, felt that reality drain away like the blood had drained from the shell of the woman in front of her. Like Cynthia, Graham bled her dry. But he kept speaking, even as he had wrung her out, and then his words filled her with a new reality, a new understanding, a new purpose.

She had planned to come here and kill Cynthia.

Graham had come instead and, with artful grace and precision, he had altered the reality of Cynthia's world. And now, using only words as his knives, he cut away and reshaped Tess.

Somewhere in that hour of words and paradigm shifts in understanding, Tess realized that Graham was more than just another person. He was worlds. He was multitudes. He was the shaper of truths.

Tess realized that she would live and die at his wish. And she realized she wanted this more than anything she had ever desired in her entire life.

In that hour, standing in front of the savaged shell of the woman he'd fucked and murdered, she fell madly, deeply, and forever in love with Graham.

His hands were hot at her sides as, when his words ultimately stopped, she turned to face him. They stared at each other for a long moment. In that moment, that eternity of time, the seed he had carefully planted over the past hour sprouted.

They kissed. There was no hesitancy, no awkwardness. Their lips met and their desire bloomed. There was a heat there, a hunger for each to feel the other, to know the other. Their hands were on each other, pressing, touching, caressing, and it wasn't enough, not enough.

Graham was the first to pull back, separating regretfully. Their breaths came in pants, their eyes were wild.

"We need to do something," he said. "We need to...mark this."

Tess thought she knew exactly what he meant, and she was ahead of him, reaching for the top button of her blouse, but he placed soft but firm hands on her. "No," he said and she heard the hurt and regret in his voice at having to stop her. "That will come. Very soon." He huffed out a breath and she knew what he meant in that single exhalation of air. *It needs to come very soon, or we'll both explode.* He wasn't wrong.

"I want to do something else first."

She didn't disagree. How could she?

NOW

TESS REMEMBERS THE stillness of the room, the quiet as Graham just seemed to study Cynthia, silently determining how they might mark this.

"May I make a suggestion," Tess remembers saying. Graham still was carrying some caution when it came to her, despite the kiss, despite the heat, still, he turned to her, eyebrows raised.

"To mark it," Tess had said, in that stinking, holy room, "you mean you want something to remember this by, correct?"

He nodded, still saying nothing. Tess still remembers that intense, youthful face, so many decades in the past.

"Then take her eyes, Graham," Tess had said, and she'd put all the passion she could into those words. "Take the eyes of the one who couldn't see you as you should be seen. The eyes of one who couldn't see the world as it should be seen."

Graham remained still for a moment, just staring into her eyes. Tess, if she closes her eyes even now, today, under this tree, can still feel the heat of that gaze.

She remembers thinking she'd said too much.

Then Graham's lips curled into that smile they were made for.

"That's perfect," he had said.

And God, how she'd wanted him right then.

1969

IN BED AFTERWARD, back in her apartment, with their sweat and his seed drying on them, Tess reached over and pulled a thin box from between her mattress and box spring. She opened it and pulled a perfectly rolled joint from the box, as well as a silver lighter- "Dad probably rolls over in his grave every time I spark a doob," she said—and lit up. She took a huge pull then offered it to Graham.

They smoked that one, and one more, and they talked of many things. The genius of Tolkien and Carlos Castaneda and Timothy Leary. The stupidity of Vietnam. The wonder of the Beatles and the Moody Blues.

And then Graham said, "Why her?"

"Who?"

"Cynthia." He pushed himself up and rested on his elbows. She swirled a finger in his damp chest hair. "Why'd you want to kill her?"

"Ugh," she said, and flopped back on her pillow. "How many ways do I loathe thee? Let me count the ways." She held up a fist, popped a finger, pushed it back with the other finger. "She's so damned awkward."

"Oh yeah?"

"Yeah. I mean, she can't really look anyone in the face, let alone the eye, when she talks to them. She's all…" Tess shifted her eyes down and to the right, then to the left, then to the right again.

"Furtive?"

"It looks that way, but it's just goddamn awkward."

"Okay, what else?"

"She's hypercritical of everyone."

"Says the woman who just judged her 'damned awkward'."

"Hey," she said, and lightly punched his shoulder. He was lean, but muscular. "Whose side are you on?"

"I'm just pointing out the obvious here."

"Anyway," she said, ignoring him. "No one, and I mean not even me, her best friend, could live up to her specifications." She huffed a sarcastic laugh. "Hell, that's why we didn't talk to you last night, so I guess that one serves her right, huh?"

"Anything else?"

"Stupid haircut that did nothing for her face. Bitching about her figure while she's pounding back a thousand calories of ice cream. Her worship of both Bobby Goldsboro and the 1910 Fruitgum Company—seriously, she had terrible taste in music. And she loves Nixon. Seriously. Do I need to go on?"

"But why did you decide that today was the day?"

"I don't know, Graham. I'm being honest here." She took another drag, her brows knitted in concentration. She blew the smoke back out, then said, "I just dropped her off last night and thought, I gotta get away from her, she's dragging me down."

Graham nodded, but stayed quiet. She put a hand on his chest. She found she felt better when she was in contact with him.

"Then, this morning, I was thinking, I'll go over and just pull the plug, but then all I could think of was how she'd be all weird and shit, and how I'd have to deal with phone calls for the next few months before she finally got the hint, and I just didn't want to go through that crap, you know? So, I changed my definition of 'pull the plug'."

"And then I showed up."

"And then you showed up," she said, lightly slapping his chest with each word.

"And screwed it all up."

"Way I see it, you did me a favour."

"Huh." He took the joint from her, pulled on it, and the room was quiet enough for Tess to hear the faint crackle of the rolling paper as it burned, to hear the smoke inhaled into his lungs. He held it for a long count of ten, then let it out slowly, savouring its release.

"So, he said, "who would you do?"

Tess laughed and gently prodded his still-mostly-hard penis with a finger. "I think I just did you."

He laughed in return and Tess enjoyed how, only hours after first meeting, despite a reasonably rocky start, they had already fallen into a comfortable conversational rhythm. "I mean, I guess I took away your target. So, who would you kill now?"

Tess lit up another joint and took a deep drag as she considered his question.

"Well, Nixon, of course. Chairman Mao. Not crazy about that Yoko Ono chick Lennon's hanging out with now. She's weird. So is Warhol for all of that, but probably not enough to kill."

"Okay," he said. "Not bad choices, but not what I was thinking." She felt an immediate pang of concern. She'd disappointed him. He continued.

"There was this kid a few years back when I was in high school. Clifton MacPherson." He paused, took a toke. Held it. Let it out. "Clifton fucking MacPherson."

She watched his face and was fascinated with his sudden intensity. She knew he was no longer here. He was years away.

"He was this overconfident kid who always bugged me about my clothes, my haircut, anytime he happened to see the book I was reading—usually an Arthur C. Clarke or Ray Bradbury. But most of all, he constantly ripped me, called me 'homo' and 'fag' for my perceived lack of interest in girls."

"You didn't seem to have any issues twenty minutes ago, tiger."

He turned to her then, and though the words were blunt, his tone was soft. "Please don't patronize me, okay?"

"Okay, Graham," she said. "I'm sorry. I just...I don't know what to say."

"I wasn't good with girls in high school." He sighed. "I'm still not, truth be told. I have no issue holding a knife to someone's throat, but just trying to talk to someone..."

"Like you were trying to do last night?"

"Yeah."

"And we ignored you."

"Yeah."

"Graham," she said. "I'm so, so sorry."

He went quiet for a while and she thought she might have lost him.

He said, "Yeah, I'd definitely kill him. I'd like to find him…I'd kill him. No problem."

"So," she said, seeing her chance, "let's look him up."

He glanced over at her, one eyebrow raised, saying nothing.

"Seriously, if someone does you wrong, if someone deserves it, no matter how long it takes, well…why not?" she said. "Let's find him and, if it can be done, let's do him. Let's kill Clifton fucking MacPherson."

NOW

TESS SITS IN the chair under the tree and smiles at the memory. *Oh yes,* she thought, *I could surprise you, couldn't I, Graham?*

1969

IT TURNED OUT to be remarkably easy to find Clifton fucking MacPherson. He was in the phone book.

Tess and Graham continued to learn more about each other through the week, spending all their time together. And, in the evenings, they drove the fifteen minutes across town to MacPherson's crappy little home. He often arrived home late, after ten. He usually had take-out or pizza with him and no one else ever came or went from the house.

"He lives alone," Graham said.

"Makes it easier," Tess said.

They made their plans for the following weekend.

Clifton fucking MacPherson didn't know it yet, but he only had a couple of days to live.

NOW

TESS TAKES ANOTHER sip of coffee, grimacing at how cool it has grown, and returns it to rest on her thigh. It's okay. Gabriela will be out soon with another cup.

I wonder what you would have done differently, you sad little man, she wonders. *If you knew you only had a little time left on God's green Earth, would you have tried to spice it up a little? Try anchovies on that last pizza? Try and find a woman and get laid? Or a man? Both?*

She chuckles to herself. *What would any of us do? Would we sit and regret our lives? Or would we try to finally live?*

Another chuckle as she looks down at her cup. *Or would we just sit under a lovely tree while our coffee grows cold?*

1969

GRAHAM WENT AROUND to the back of MacPherson's house, looking for a basement window to break and enter through. Instead, he found the most pathetic attempt to repair a broken window he'd ever seen.

"It's a basement window, man. Anyone with half a brain knows you wouldn't use cardboard." He pulled at the soggy cardboard and duct tape that had long ago offered its power to stick up to the weather gods. The cold moist material felt slimy and he quickly tossed it under an overgrown hedge to the side and climbed in.

Inside, it was worse. There had to be an inch of water in the basement, and it smelled like a backed-up sewer down here. Small things bobbed as he slogged through the mess. One was a doll's head, separated from its body.

A doll? He stood, the cold water soaking into his shoes and socks, as he considered that. *But no one else lives here.*

Then the mess and the lackluster attempts at home repair made more sense. *She left you. She left you and she took your daughter with her*. He toed the doll's head and it rolled in the water, its vacant eyes closing.

"We're gonna be doing you as much of a favour as we did for Cynthia," he said, but low, under his breath.

He found the stairs and made his way up and to the side door. He unlocked it quietly, taking his time, and let Tess in, enjoying the expectation betrayed by her raised eyebrows. Behind her, the morning sun was pinkening the sky, but had not yet broken over the landscape.

He closed the door just as quietly.

Then, from behind him.

"What the fuck you doing in my house?"

1969

CLIFTON FUCKING MACPHERSON stood a couple of steps above the main floor, having come down from the upper level. He had on a pair of tighty-whities barely holding on under a big round belly, and a dirty bathrobe. His eyes were bleary from just coming out of sleep, and the impressions of the pillow were still carved into his cheek.

His hair was pillow-flattened on one side, and thinning enough that, despite the good-sized frizz of curly hair, the top of his head was easily visible. There was a lot of grey in his porkchop sideburns and stubbly chin. Bags under the eyes.

Clifton fucking MacPherson looked like shit.

Almost bad enough that Graham considered leaving him to his misery, because death would probably be kinder.

MacPherson squinted. "I know you." He waggled a finger at Graham. "You're that Williamson faggot, aren't you? Gay-ham."

"Jesus," Graham said. "Seriously? After all these years?"

"Graham," Tess said, and he caught the note of warning in her voice.

"That cunt your beard?"

Graham didn't think. He reacted, crossed the room in four long strides. MacPherson, for his part, awkwardly turned and tried to gallop up the steps, but he'd only climbed two when Graham's blade whickered out and left two deep gashes in the backs of his knees.

MacPherson fell on his face and slid down the stairs.

Graham grabbed a handful of bathrobe and hauled MacPherson, now mewling in pain, over on his back.

"You can spew all the shit you want about me, Cliff, but you will not talk about the woman I love like that."

Then Graham stuffed his hand in MacPherson's mouth, wrenched down on his jaw until he heard a sharp double pop that signaled dislocation. He nodded grimly, then took hold of his bully's waggling, drooling tongue and hacked it away from its roots.

NOW

THE WOMAN I love, he'd said. He'd said he loved her, and he said it while defending her honour. Then he'd cut out MacPherson's tongue so he could speak no more evil.

It was in that second, Tess remembers under the wonderful old tree, that she knew she loved him too. It was a stone of certainty in her, something that had weight.

When he turned to her with MacPherson's tongue in his hand, the tongue that had made an enemy of Graham, she watched as it dripped with spit and blood.

And, with the expectant look on Graham's face, the frantic mewling of the hobbled MacPherson behind him, and his tongue dripping on to his dirty carpet, Tess remembers feeling the answering gush of wet from herself.

"Bind him, Graham," she said, her voice husky and unrecognizable to herself.

He did. Tess, eighty years old and more than fifty years removed from the event, feels a stirring even now as she remembers Graham turning around, seeing his look first of surprise, then lust as she stands before him in this horrible, decrepit house, naked.

Yes, Tess has no problem bringing up the memories and the feelings, the lust and the love.

1969

"BABY," SHE SAID. Graham looked up from what he was doing, his face wet with her. He'd already given her one good orgasm, but she wanted more.

She said, "We need to…do what we came to do. Please."

Maybe it was the tremor in her voice. Maybe it was the tremor in her thighs, but Graham seemed to instantly understand.

NOW

WHAT THEY DID to Clifton fucking MacPherson was horrible, vile. Things Tess didn't even know she was capable of thinking, let alone carrying out.

It took a long time for MacPherson to die.

And that was okay.

But what came next…

1969

THE DIRTY RUG sponged up everything the inside of MacPherson could give it. MacPherson was virtually unrecognizable as a once-living human being. He was meat and organs and bone and blood.

So much blood.

Tess became intoxicated by it. The sharp metallic smell filled her lungs and tightened her nipples. The warmth and wet and stickiness of the blood underfoot made her legs weak.

Graham turned to her as she sat down on the sopping wet rug, her hands supporting her as she leaned back. "You okay?" he said.

She spread her legs, then, with one bloody hand, spread her sex for him. "I'm fine," she said.

He moved toward her and she reached up and pulled his fly down slowly, the blood smearing the front of his pants. He watched her.

She undid the belt buckle, then the clasp on his pants. "Pull them down."

He did, never taking his eyes off hers. Her other hand was busy working herself. "I am so fucking turned on right now," she said.

When his cock was free, she reached up with both hands, slick with MacPherson's blood, and she worked his cock, sliding one hand over his hardness as the other played with his balls.

His head fell back as he whispered, "oh my god, Tess."

Then she took his bloodied cock into her mouth. She felt his balls tighten and knew he was close, so she just held him there, tasting his sweat, the blood.

She released him and eased him down between her legs, his cock jumping with his pulse.

"Fuck me," she said. "Fuck me in that asshole's blood."

Graham fucked her.

And this time, when she came, he came with her, and it was spectacular.

They had found each other.

1969

THAT WAS THEIR first murder together. Afterward, they found MacPherson's heart—Graham making the comment that he was surprised there was one to be found—and put it in a Tupperware

MacPherson had in his kitchen. For good measure, Tess took his balls and tossed them in too.

"What are we going to do with this?" Tess said.

"Same thing we do with Cynthia's eyes."

"And what's that?"

"Haven't worked that out yet," Graham said. "Are we going to do this again?"

"Kill someone?"

"Yes."

"Are we going to…" Tess looked over at the blood smeared around the room. "Are we going to do that again, too?"

Graham smiled. "I would hope so."

"Then the answer's yes," Tess said. "Yes, we are going to do this again."

He hefted the Tupperware container. "Then we need to commemorate this… somehow."

"What have you got in mind?"

"Like I said, not sure yet. No idea, really," he said. "But we're creative. We'll think of something."

"Let's think about it after we clean up," Tess said. "What do you think the chances are that Clifton fucking MacPherson's tub is clean?"

1969

THEY CLEANED THEMSELVES up in MacPherson's filthy bathroom, then they cleaned up after themselves. It was early afternoon when they got back to Tess's apartment and they had a longer shower this time. Then they fell into Tess's too tiny bed and slept the afternoon away.

When they awoke, they found they were ravenous. They hit a takeout, then went to Graham's for a change of clothes. Then they went for a drive.

Tess said, "Where we headed?"

"Pick a direction."

She hooked a thumb out the passenger window. "Into the sun, my good man," she said. "Into the sun."

Graham spun the wheel left and into the sun.

NOW

TESS WATCHES AS her daughter Gabriela walks across the field, coffees precariously held in one hand, a folding lawn chair in the other.

Ella has so much of Graham in her, it causes Tess some pain to see her. In her early forties, with kids of her own, she was a striking woman. It gives Tess comfort to know that, once she is gone, the family businesses will continue for at least another generation.

She reaches Tess and drops the chair. Tess takes the proffered coffees. "You don't need to bring a chair, Ella, there's a perfectly fine one right there." She nods toward the empty one.

"Nope," she says, "that's Dad's." She unfolds her lawn chair and sits down. Tess hands her cup back.

They both gaze at the empty chair as they sip in an easy silence, each in their own thoughts.

1969

TWENTY MINUTES LATER, they were well west of the city, and in a mesh of county roads dividing the rolling hills into neat squares.

"So much nicer out here, isn't it?" Tess said, her chin on her arm, her face in the evening wind.

"Really is," Graham said. "I'd move out here in a heartbeat."

"Me too," she said. "Buy a big stretch of land with a big old drafty house, then spend a bunch of years renovating it, room by room."

"Yeah," he said. "I could get behind that. If, you know, we were rich."

Tess gave him a long, penetrating look. Then he watched her turn back to the window, but her eyes were downcast, seeing nothing. Deep in thought.

He let her mind drift, keeping quiet. Instead, he stole glances at her. Lean, soft features that disguised the sharp mind. Innocent eyes that hid the wanton heart. Long-fingered hands that concealed claws.

To think he'd come close to killing her.

That would have been such a waste.

He watched the road, happy with the thought that he hadn't stilled all the thoughts in that head.

1969

"GRAHAM," SHE SAID. "Stop."

He looked around, but there wasn't much to see. It was almost dark now, and they were on a dirt road that apparently led nowhere. There was nothing really on either side of them, aside from an abandoned home in serious disrepair off in the distance, and an empty field that stretched for miles.

As he slowed the vehicle down and pulled off to the shoulder, he noticed that wasn't quite right. The field wasn't completely empty. One lonely tree stood forlornly in the middle of it all, a lost child, waiting for its mother to come and take it back home.

Tess pointed to the tree. "There," she said.

"The tree?"

"Yes."

Graham shrugged his shoulders, shut the car off, looked at the excitement in her face and said, "Okay. What do we need?"

"Just a shovel and a flashlight."

Of course, he had both in the trunk. He fetched the tools while she grabbed the grocery bag with the Tupperware in it.

There wasn't even a fence to hop, so they walked through the tall rustling grass until they got to the tree.

It wasn't much to look at, this tree. Maybe ten feet tall, slender trunk. Graham didn't know trees, only knew maples from their leaves, and birches from their bark. Beyond that, he was hopeless. From the few leaves on this scabby thing, it was definitely a maple.

Tess bent to the tree and brushed away some leaves to clear a small patch of earth. "Let's bury him here. This tree will feed on his wicked heart and his useless balls, and turn something awful into something beautiful."

Graham smiled at her as she rose, brushing dirt from her hands.

"Should we bring Cynthia here to watch over him, too?"

"I think we should, yes."

He kissed her then, lightly, softly, then said, "Okay, Tess."

Then he went to work.

NOW

TESS SITS UNDER that same tree, all these years later, and remembers watching Graham. He'd stopped halfway in and pulled off his shirt, and she remembers the flex and pull of his muscles as he worked. Remembers how the moonlight made the sheen of sweat on his shoulders and back shine.

Her fingers twitch with the memory of the plastic of the container with MacPherson's mortal remains inside. His black heart and his useless balls.

When Graham was finished, they would deliver him back to the earth.

Tess sips at her coffee, gives Ella a smile and gets one in return, and remembers the two of them, in this very spot, so long ago, him in the hole he'd dug, her standing above, watching him.

But as she watched him, as she took in the land around them, Tess remembers something just clicking in her young, overly-optimistic mind.

She looks up at the tree, its branches high above her, MacPherson's parts buried long ago below her, and she smiles at that decades old flash of insight that set the course for the rest of their lives.

"The whole shebang," she says, the smile never leaving her face.

Ella just smiles.

She's heard the stories. *The whole shebang*. She knows.

1969

"I'VE FIGURED IT out," Tess said.

Graham pulled himself up out of the hole in the ground. "Figured out what, Tess?"

"All of it," she said, throwing her arms wide. "Everything. The whole shebang."

"You're gonna have to give me a little more to go on," he said, swiping the dirt from his arms.

So, Tess explained.

NOW

TESS REMEMBERS, AS she looks toward the house she and Graham shared for decades, the house her daughter grew up in. She angles her view across the expanse of their land, remembers how it was that night long ago, when only the one tree she sat under now had occupied the empty field.

Now, the land was forested with trees. Each one with a story behind it.

Now, the one who was with her is gone, but their daughter is here in his place. One story almost finished, another well on its way.

Tess's plan had been simple in concept, much more difficult to execute…if they were going to kill, then they had to kill those that could help them.

Money. Money was the Great Eraser. As easy as Graham and Tess could wipe out a life, money could wipe their debts. It could wipe their misfortunes. It could wipe the second life from those who should never see it, while also buying the public one everyone would need to see.

Yes, they needed to choose their victims with less emotion and more research.

And, over the next few years, that's what they did, traveling as needed, staying in out-of-the way one-star motels that appreciated cash and asked no questions. They would observe, plan, and do what needed to be done. Those kills were their job.

And each time they did, a piece of that person would come back with them to the tree farm, and another tree would be planted. And the money they got, the possessions and things that could be sold or bartered away, the wealth they very quickly accumulated, it all went into first the small parcel of land they bought. The one with that lone tree. Over the years, as more and more land came available around them, they bought it up.

In between, they still had their fun, still found those that needed revenge killing. Those kills, with the inevitable carnal, blood-soaked sex afterward, were their fun.

The money killings were their job. The other killings were their passion.

They were able to retire from their job by the time Tess found out she was pregnant with Gabriela, late in 1981.

Then they had many passions. Their little girl. The trees. And killing those that had, for one reason or another, forfeited their joy for life with pettiness, hate, greed, or simple small-mindedness.

Graham and Tess looked at them as souls who had one last purpose in life, and that was to feed their passions, to offer up their blood to Tess and Graham's carnal desires, and a small piece of themselves to the garden, where they could continue to be useful, long after they'd been forgotten by the few people who harbored any memories of them.

There were a lot of trees planted since 1969.

They kept killing, but slowed the pace by 1980. They were killers, sure, but they killed those that had earned it. It was a drag when Lennon was shot, and it took some of the fun out of their own killings.

So, they had a baby.

And they chose their targets more sparingly, but carefully, each one planned like others would plan a vacation.

And they kept planting trees.

It was a good life and a fun ride.

THREE MONTHS AGO

THEN CAME THE day when the wheels fell off their perfect ride.

Three months ago, Graham couldn't get out of bed. His back was aching so bad, he couldn't move.

Tess and Ella got him to the hospital, who's so-called professionals did nothing for him beyond a quick examination and a snap diagnosis based primarily on his advanced age, then sent Graham on his way, a prescription for muscle relaxants in a pocket.

Two days later, he was back. Tests were run. Scans were run. Then more tests. More scans. A biopsy. A second biopsy.

Cancer.

Undiagnosed prostate cancer that had slithered its way into Graham's bones as well as through far too much of his soft tissue.

The standard warnings soon followed. "We can keep him comfortable, but there's nothing we could do to save him." He had weeks, at best.

Through it all, Graham was stoic, and Tess remained supportive. It was what it was.

Both of them knew that they'd dealt enough death out that, sooner or later, the deal would shift, and one of them would pick up the wrong card.

Everyone had an end date. Graham's was coming sooner than expected.

TWO DAYS AGO

SHE NEVER DISCUSSED it with him. Stuff like this, they never did.

Stuff like this. The very personal, *this is me* stuff. If it involved them both, yes, they talked it all out. But Tess was going to be the one left behind. This was one of those *this is me* things that she had to work out on her own.

Waiting for Graham as he spent endless hours in endless waiting rooms, labs, and doctors' offices, she had a lot of time to think it through. Tess had always been a meticulous planner, and this particular situation—not the specifics, but more the, *what if something happens that he's debilitated* sort of thing—was one of the many scenarios she'd considered over the decades.

She had long ago determined the *what* of her plan. It was the *how* that now consumed her thoughts and, once that was determined, the *when*.

It took a bit, but she worked it out. Tess always did.

THIS MORNING

GRAHAM HAD COME home. "I'm not dying in some damned hospital, Tess." She, of course, agreed. It would have been the same for her, had their situations been reversed.

She got him out of their bed—he'd flat-out refused the hospital bed at home option—and wheeled him and his IVs out to the kitchen, where the sun offered up its best light. She parked him by the big oak table, the smell of the brewing coffee filling the air.

She didn't have to ask. Once she set the locks on the wheelchair, she got two mugs down, poured the coffee and fixed them the way they both liked them.

She placed Graham's in his outstretched hands, and he managed to take it without spilling it from the shakes. It was a little win, but they'd take it.

She sat, and they made small talk for a bit, waiting for Ella to make her way out. It was nice, spending the time talking about unimportant stuff, everyday trivial details. For a few minutes, Tess could forget the cancerous elephant in the room, forget that the man she'd spent the vast majority of her life with, the one that knew almost all her secrets, would be gone shortly.

Ella came in, bent and gave her father a kiss on his cheek, got her own cup of coffee and refilled theirs.

NOW

"YOU GONNA BE okay, Mom?"

Tess, for the first time not really trusting her voice, just nods. But then she realizes, she has a question that needs to be asked. She takes a longer pull on the coffee—now at the perfect temperature—swallows, then reaches out a hand, placing it over her daughter's.

"How about you, hon?" she says. "You gonna be okay?"

The tears brim in Ella's eyes, but she just as quickly swipes them away. "I'm fine. I'll be fine." She nods. And Tess knows she will. Graham and her, they'd done a good job raising their only child. Gabriela was strong.

Tess nods back, gives her daughter's hand one last squeeze. "I love you," she says. "Your dad loves you, too."

Ella says a soft, "I know," and stands. She picks up the folding chair and her mug, leaving Tess's with her. "I'll get everything ready."

"Okay, Ella," Tess says. "Okay."

And then she's alone again.

Just her, the empty chair, and the tree.

She takes another long pull on the coffee.

THIS MORNING

THE NEXT HALF-HOUR went by in both pleasant conversation and comfortable silences, each of the three simply enjoying each other's company, and the simple pleasure of a quiet morning with no place to be.

At some point during one of those silences, Ella glanced over to her mother, and Tess gave her a slight nod. Ella rose. "Want anything else, Dad?" she said, and Graham declined with a smile. Ella rinsed her cup and placed it in the dishwasher.

"I'm gonna go get some stuff ready," she said, then gave her father one last lingering kiss on the top of his head. Tess watched her as she closed her eyes and brought a hand up to lightly stroke his hair. "Love you, old man," she said.

"Love you too, young lady," he said back.

Then Ella was gone.

Tess got up and repeated her daughter's actions, rinsing and racking her cup. But instead of returning to her seat, she pulled something from a drawer, then moved behind Graham.

Then, she placed the blade against his throat.

Graham didn't react much. She saw a hand lift, as though to reach for it, but then he dropped it back to his lap.

"Oh how the situation has reversed, hasn't it, Tess?"

"It has."

"Was this always the plan?"

"No, babe," she said. "If I was going to go before you, I just would have gone. But with you going first—"

"You can take your revenge."

She said nothing, just held the blade close to his throat.

He huffed out a small laugh. "Was it something I said?"

Tess laughed as well. "Like Mom always said, 'looks'll fade, but a sense of humour?'"

"'That's forever'," Graham finished.

"Yeah."

"Yeah," he said, then sighed. "Forever, less a few days, I guess."

That made her sad, but she had to get through this.

"Like you said, Graham, the situation has reversed. You were where I am, you held a knife to my throat, and you were going to kill me."

"I understand that revenge is a dish best served cold, but Tess…fifty years? It's gone past cold, past stale, to rancid."

"You taught me, Graham," Tess said, "that it's a good thing to make people pay for past actions, no matter how long it takes."

"Clifton fucking MacPherson."

"Exactly."

"And what—"

"That night," Tess said. "In the bar. You sent the drinks over."

"And you didn't acknowledge."

"And, instead of coming over to us, you sent the drinks over. Instead of giving me a little time, you left. Then you fucked and killed Cynthia, and were prepping to do the same to me."

"I—"

"Tell me I'm wrong, Graham."

Graham remained stoic for a moment, then lowered his head slightly. "No, you're not wrong."

"Thank you for that."

"So, was this all a lie, then?"

"No, I've loved you almost since the beginning, Graham. You lowered your knife, then you lowered your guard, and I was yours." She applied the smallest amount of pressure to the knife at his neck. "But I never forgot your original intent."

"And what happens now?"

"I'm going to slash open your throat, Graham. You'll bleed out very quickly. The knife is extremely sharp, so there shouldn't be too much pain."

"I know you know this, Tess, but I never wanted to waste away. God knows, we've meted out both quick and slow deaths over the years. I always wanted mind to be quick. So this?" He pauses, raises one hand to lightly touch hers, holding the knife, then lets it fall again. "All in all, not a bad way to go."

"No."

"And then?"

"And then I'll bury you under our tree." She smiled. "On the opposite side to Clifton fucking MacPherson's balls."

"And Cynthia's unworthy eyes."

"Yes," Tess said, "and Cynthia's unworthy eyes, too."

"Thank you for that," he said.

"Are you ready?"

She watched her husband close his eyes and take a deep breath. He turned to face her, opened his eyes and met hers and said, "Two things. First, I'm sorry we met the way we did. If I could go back and change it, please know that I would."

Tess nodded.

"And second, I'm honoured that it will be you that spills my blood and claims my life. Now that it's here, I wouldn't have it any other way."

He turned his head away from her.

"You're ready?"

"I love you, Tess."

"I love you too, Graham."

Then she opened his throat.

NOW

TESS DRAINS HER coffee, feeling the weariness creeping in.

Ella is such a good daughter, helping her clean the mess she'd made killing her husband, the kitchen smelling only fresh and clean afterward. She'd used the tractor and got the hole dug. She'd helped Tess get Graham's empty husk down to the floor of the hole and lay him out. She'd made Tess's final coffee, the one with the extra ingredient.

And it would be Ella who would come after to finish things up.

But right now, it's up to Tess to get herself down. She knows she doesn't have long.

She stands, and a wave of dizziness washes over her, like the lightheadedness when standing too fast with low blood pressure, something she'd had earlier in life.

Holding on to the chair as long as possible, she works around it to the hole just behind her. She carefully positions a foot on a rung of the ladder, then the other, one step down.

Then she stops.

"I may have waited too long." She'd hoped to get to the bottom with some dignity intact, but Ella may find her sprawled at the bottom instead.

Still, she grips the ladder tight with both hands, and remembers the sheen of sweat on Graham's back by this tree all those decades ago. She clings to the memory like she does to the ladder, and makes her way slowly and carefully down the rungs, pausing only twice more to allow the dizziness to pass.

Her limbs feel boneless by the time she reaches the bottom, like rubber. She gratefully sits down beside her husband, his body wrapped in white sheets, only his face open. His eyes are closed and, except for the bloodless pale of his skin, he could be sleeping.

But no, there's no rise and fall of the chest. No beating of his heart.

And Tess had known since that first night with him, she couldn't face another day on this earth without the beating of that heart, so entwined with hers.

She stretches out and, as she had done almost every night of their life together, Tess puts one leg across Graham's, wraps her arm around his waist, and puts her head on his chest.

"It was a good life, baby, wasn't it?" she says. Then, quieter, "I love you, Graham."

Then, as the drugs take full effect, Tess first sleeps, comforted that this resting place, this final place of peace is both the first and the last tree in their garden.

It takes no time at all for Tess to fall as still and silent as her partner.

STORY NOTES

I SORT OF know where this one comes from, and sort of don't.

Gotta say, sometimes social media gives us some wild conversations to sit back and watch unfold. Most are just interesting, but sometimes… sometimes, as a writer, I hit pay dirt.

The weird, sex-in-the-fresh-blood came from a social media conversation that I witnessed many years back. Basically one person was trying to justify that if they murdered someone, fucking in their blood was the best way to honour them…or something to that effect. I'm not sure, nor did I care to look at their justifications too closely.

But the idea stuck in my mind as something that might find a home someday in one of my stories.

Often, as I carry these odd little things around in the basement of my mind, I just wait for some other weird thing to get tossed carelessly in the basement, and maybe it smacks up against something else and causes a spark.

I also had this other unfocused germ of an idea. This whole boyfriend/girlfriend or husband/wife set of serial killers that came from—I think—a combination of the hold Manson had on his followers, as well as the creepy Canadian duo of Paul Bernardo and Karla Homolka, utter monsters who did their business within about an hour's drive of me and, for their crimes, they now both live in relative safety and luxury. Just goes to show you, folks, you want to retire and live easy, just kill a few people and let the Canadian Legal System set you up for life afterward.

Anyway, somehow, this serial killer duo and the sex in blood fetish ideas leaked together. Don't ask me where the tree stuff came from. No idea.

Originally, I started this story for the *NEFARIAM: THE ELEMENT OF CRIME* anthology that we—that is, me and my ID Press buddies—were producing, but I soon realized it was going to be far too long for the collection, so I set it aside and worked on a different story instead. That other story came to be known as *The Riff* and you can find it in *UGLY STORIES, VOL. 2.*

After I wrapped up that second story, every so often this one would float back up in my mind like a corpse washing up on a beach, and it was one of those rare stories where I had the title almost immediately. Typically I tie myself in knots trying to come up with a title, but not this one.

So, fairly quickly, I had my serial killer team, and when it came time to get the two of them started, enter Clifton fucking MacPherson. I went to school with the real version of this fictional person. Obviously, I'm not gonna seek out the real-life guy that made the 1976/77 school year shitty for me and, as the kids say, unalive him.

But could I get my revenge in a story? Hell yes.

One final element entered as I wrote. I wondered if I could, on some small level, make these two psychopaths somehow a little sympathetic. I'm not sure if I succeeded, nor am I sure I truly wanted to, but it was an interesting experiment to try.

Either way, love or hate Graham and Tess, I hope you at least dug the story.

CHANGE OF HEART

"HERE WE ARE."

Michelle follows the group into the nightclub like a panther stepping into a cage in a zoo. She is the last of the group of six women, the other five already starting to move their bodies to the beat of the song playing at a volume designed for permanent auditory damage.

One of them—her name might be Kate—puts her mouth close to Michelle's ear and yells, "This is gonna be so much fun!"

Michelle gives her most polite smile, leaving her disagreement unspoken. Kate scoots back to the main group. *Women these days,* Michelle thinks, then scolds herself. *You are one of them now, Shelley.*

Four of them angle left for drinks, leaving Kate and Michelle the job of finding a table.

The two of them move deeper into the room. It's all lights and noise and sweat and various odours and bodies in violent, rhythmic motion.

And Michelle wonders, not for the last time, *why am I here?*

HERE WE ARE. I'm not surprised to watch you walk in, the last in the group of six, the muted one at the end of the line. I knew you'd be here.

My heart told me you would. I've learned to trust it.

There's an entire room full of strangers separating us. Probably better, at least to start. You can't see me from here. Nor do you want to, I'm sure.

But I can see you.

And that's enough.

For now.

GODS DAMN IT! They drag her here, then leave her. They had sworn they would not, but even as they had promised, she'd known they would. Even as the four others rejoin her and Kate with various sweating drinks clutched in slippery hands, she'd known they were going to abandon her.

They'd all dutifully sat down at the table, but with conversation virtually impossible over the *OONSE! OONSE! OONSE!* beat of the music, the women she is with look like leashed dogs, their eyes glancing quickly but longingly at the dancefloor as one great old song after another comes on.

Apparently, their limit is the extended dance track version of Blondie's *Heart of Glass*. "Just this one song, Shell!" Trudy yells. "Come on! Dance with us."

Michelle uses the same polite smile again, and shakes her head no. Trudy gives her a somewhat sad and mostly unreadable look, but nods and the five women stand and move toward the writhing bodies, leaving Michelle on her own to guard the drinks.

She knows Trudy has the best of intentions. This past year has not been good and, though Michelle mostly keeps to herself, Trudy knows she's been through a death and what she probably believes to be a bad breakup. *How could it be a breakup,* Michelle thinks, *when the intent had been to throw her heart away? To never see the woman, Libi, ever again?*

And even the death is nowhere near as recent as Michelle has led her friend to believe. So, Trudy's heart is in the right place.

This is Trudy's way of getting her back out in the world. And Michelle isn't sure why she said yes, because she truly has no desire to be in the world at all lately.

Just live out your days in peace, then you will no longer be in the world.

It's a good thought.

I no longer want to live. I've lived too long. I feel so dead. I should be dead.

A better thought, but a thought that's interrupted.

I STAND NEAR the wall of the club, a massive place that was once a supermarket, before being turned into a multi-level bar. The DJ sits godlike, above the crowd, spinning old dance hits. Old enough to elicit groans, but nostalgically popular enough to get the bodies on the dance floor.

You don't dance, though. You're not a dancer.

And you don't look comfortable.

Reading your body language, I can tell it's your friends that dragged you out tonight. The dress you're in flatters you, as though sprayed on to your body. It highlights every curve. Your hair looks good flowing around your shoulders. You don't wear it down enough, but it frames your face to full effect, and shows off your perfect cheekbones, the arc of your jaw, your sensuous neck.

Yet, for all your beauty, you look only at the glasses on the small table. Your hands fidget with your hair, or the thin necklace, or the stem of the glass.

My heart goes out to you. You don't want to be here. It's obvious and, if your companions were true friends, they'd see that.

I see that.

Some pressure cooker shambles over to me, his hair artfully messed, with a radius of body spray odour that's far too thick to be healthy. He performs his desultory, pre-scripted, one-size-fits-all come on for me, and I politely turn him down.

He visibly musters himself for a second, stronger attempt and I'm less polite the second time. The pressure cooker calls me a "lesbo bitch" and shambles off, in search of an easier conquest.

I don't want to be here. I came for you.

Because, where you are, Michelle, I will be, too.

I can't stay away, even though you want me to. My heart won't let me.

I pull away from the wall and move toward you.

And I can feel the thumping of my heart in my chest.

I feel so alive.

♦♦♦

"HEY," HE SAYS. "How you doing?"

"Whatever or however I'm doing," Michelle answers, "I prefer to do it alone."

"Hey," the guy says with a grin—Michelle is sure he thinks it's a winning smile—fastening itself into place on his artfully unshaven face, "it doesn't have to be like that. I just—"

Michelle holds up a hand. "Look, I'm sure you're a great guy, but..." she says, throwing up a hand to cut him off from whatever he was about to interject with, "*But* I'm not the one you're looking for, okay? There's a lot of likely prospects here tonight, I'm sure, but I'm not one of them." She meets his eyes. "Okay?"

"Okay, but—"

"But nothing, big guy."

Michelle and the guy both turn to the new person in the conversation.

"She said she's not interested. So, she's not interested."

"You again?" he says, looking her up and down. "What's this? You turn me down and now you're out to fuck up my entire night?

"No, I'm just the woman who doesn't want to have to explain how 'no means no' works. Do I need to get security over here?"

"Hey, whoa," the guy says, one hand splayed, the other precariously holding the drink while three fingers splay. "It's cool. No means no. Got it." He turns to leave, but both women catch the scowl and the muttered epithet that crosses his lips.

Michelle ignores it because her night has just become far more complicated.

Libi.

♦♦♦

I WATCH THE expression on your face sour rapidly, so I throw my Hail Mary.

"Before you send me packing like Mr. Cro-Magnon there," I say, hooking a thumb over my shoulder, "can I just talk to you? Five minutes, no more. If you don't want to hear from me again, I'm gone."

"Libi," you say, and my name feels like a kiss from your lips, "we've been through this. I don't—"

"We have," I agree, "and…we haven't. I've done a lot of thinking over the past few months and—"

"And you don't think I have too?" You drop your gaze and shake your head. I can't hear you over the throb of the music, but I can see you mouth *Jesus Christ,* and I know I'm blowing it with you.

Again.

Fuck.

"Please. Michelle." I risk putting a hand on your shoulder. You allow it a moment before you twist away, but it's a moment of hope for me.

Then, unbelievably, there's another guy coming between us.

♦♦♦

HE TURNS TO Michelle. "Excuse me, Miss. Is this woman bothering you?"

The question, though fair, takes Michelle by surprise. Enough that she has to consider it for a moment. *Is Libi bothering me?*

The answer is yes, but she hesitates to verbalise that. Instead, the bouncer obviously assumes the worst from the expression on her face. "If she's making you uncomfortable, I can—"

"No," Michelle says. "No, it's okay. We just...it's been a long time, and I'm just a little surprised to see her here, is all."

"Okay," the bouncer says, but she can tell he's not completely buying it. "Dude over there—" the bouncer points a finger at the guy from earlier who smiles and raises his glass as if in a toast to her, the fucker "—said he thought you might be in some distress."

"No," Michelle says, "I'm okay."

The bouncer gives her a long look, then shoots Libi a cold-eyed glare. He puts himself directly between Libi and Michelle, drops to one knee, and looks directly into Michelle's eyes. "If anything changes..." he holds up his hand, thumb tucked to palm, then closes his fingers down over it in the distress signal "...I'll keep an eye out, okay?"

Michelle almost tears up at this. "Thank you," she says. "Truly." Then she nods. "I'm okay."

He gives her one more long look with his kind eyes and nods. "Fair enough." He stands and moves off.

As Michelle makes a decision, Libi says

"WHAT THE FUCK was that all about?"

Instead of answering me, you stand, grab your untrendy large purse, and say, "I need to tell you a few things. Follow me."

Not exactly what I was hoping for, but I'll take what I can get.

You take my hand, and lead me out of the club.

LIBI SAYS, "WHERE are we going?"

Michelle's not sure until she sees the alleyway between a pawn shop and a restaurant across the street. All the businesses aside from the nightclub are closed, save for an all-night burrito place at the other end of the block.

"Here," she says, and leads Libi into the darkness inside the darkness of night.

"Why here?"

Michelle lets go of her hand and faces her. "Because what I need to tell you, I need to tell you privately," she says. "And I'm not going to yell over music, or have this conversation in a restroom."

Libi reaches out, as though to put her hands on Michelle's hips. Michelle gently, yet firmly, pushes them away. "We're not going there, Libi."

"Then where are we going? Because I'll follow you wherever you lead."

And that's the biggest problem, isn't it? Michelle thinks.

ALL I WANT to do is reach out to you. To hold you.

I want to pull you close, to let you feel how my heart beats for you.

You won't let me.

Instead, you back up to the far wall of the alley, and you start to talk.

And Jesus hopped-up Christ on a motorbike, what you tell me...

"I MARRIED YOUNG," Michelle says. "Far too young. I was an intelligent, yet precociously stupid girl who made some spectacular decisions, and some spectacularly bad decisions."

"Hey, we've all—"

"Don't interrupt. I need to get this out." She sighs, drops her head for a moment, then faces Libi again.

"Anyway, long story short, I fell in love with a man I probably shouldn't have. Four years later, he was dead. But...there was a wrinkle.

"The short version is, he had to be cremated. And I came to be in possession of his heart. No, do not interrupt. The details aren't important. What's important is what came in the years following that.

"I was heartbroken, of course, and I kept his heart wrapped in a poem—don't ask, it's not important—then wrapped in silk. For the longest time, it was on my desk, where I wrote and conducted all my affairs. I'd be lying if I told you I didn't unwrap it on occasion, and just hold the burned meat of the heart in my hand, just to feel a little closer to him.

"As the years passed, I pulled it out less often and then, a couple of decades on, found myself setting it away in a drawer, not because I missed him or loved him any less, but because sometimes the pain of the loss became too overwhelming.

"However, the next time I decided I needed to feel the weight of it in my hand, I opened the drawer, and I confess, I screamed.

"Because the heart was still there, still wrapped in silk and poetry, however, both were sodden, as was the drawer, in blood.

"I didn't believe it at first, couldn't believe it, and I reached in to pull the heart out...and Libi, with God as my witness, the heart was beating." She raises a palm to me. "Please, no. Don't say anything. I know how this sounds, but I have to get it all out, now that I've started." She drops her hand. "I pulled the heart out, and I felt the pulse of it in my hand. I felt its warmth. The blood that covered my palms and leaked between my fingers was warm. It was *warm*, Libi.

"I kept the poetry and the silk, but I put all of it in a large bowl and set it back in the drawer, once I'd cleaned and dried it as best I could. And, while that was strange, stranger things were to come.

"Over the next few months, I tried every way to be rid of it. Elemental ways: burning, burying, drowning. But also cutting, crushing, abandoning. Nothing worked. It was always in my drawer the next day. What could I do, but accept its constant presence in my life?

"It took only a little longer for me to notice some uncomfortable things. I began to get comments on how young I was looking, how I didn't look my age. I noticed the stares of men had become longer, uncomfortably so.

"I probably shouldn't confess this, but there was a time when I travelled to America. I met with a very famous writer—call him a kindred spirit—and we shared too much drink and too much information. Later, he published a terrifying story about a heart that was spun out of that night's conversation." She frowns. "I was displeased, but I had no one to blame, save myself.

"He was found mysteriously dead a few years later. I'll speak no more of that.

"Within a few years, it became a bigger issue as, by now, I was passing more as a younger sibling when with my children, rather than a parent. It is, once again, a much longer story that I have neither the time nor the inclination to relate. Suffice it to say, I ultimately had to move, leaving my children and my life behind. I did, however, take the heart with me.

"Yes, it was still beating.

"Having to go to such measures came only after I'd realised what was happening. I wasn't growing younger, though I did appear to for a bit. No, it was that I simply was not growing any older."

♦ ♦ ♦

AND NOW, YOU'RE scaring me. *Did you really kill someone? A famous author?*

Then I think, *No, you're trying to freak me out, you're trying to scare me off. The crazy ex that I should feel glad I escaped with my sanity and wallet intact. Or my life.*

Fair enough. I decide to just shut up and not judge anything you say.

"THIS NOT GROWING older, it goes on for…far too long. At first, while I miss my children and my life, there's also a remarkable freedom in starting over, in reinventing yourself. So, once I realize that this is what I must do, I embrace it.

"And, for a long time, as I say, it's wonderful. I travel to Italy. Then Spain. Then France. I travel to even more remote locations, and I see all the wonders this world has to offer.

"Of course, the biggest wonder of this world is the one that is with me. The beating heart that keeps me ageless. There is a long period of time where I become quite suspicious of others. Do they also have their own wondrous secrets? There must be. Yet that realisation also terrifies me.

"I retreat from my fellow man, and a horrible *ennui* sets in. I am at a loss as to how to continue.

"Then, providence intervenes."

♦ ♦ ♦

NOT GONNA LIE, I'm beginning to weary of this, and I'm hoping you wrap this up, or come to your point soon. So much for keeping this story short.

Because now it's getting ridiculous. Are you trying to scare me off, or are you off your meds?

For all your madness, you won't get rid of me that easily.

"I'M BORING you, aren't I? I can see by the clenching of your jaw. Fine, I'll increase the pace.

"There is a night where I am—unwisely, it turns out—walking down a dark street, much like the one out there, when I am attacked. It's cold. Mid-November, I remember, and at the time I lived in London. I should have known better, there'd been five horrible murders in the previous couple of months.

"Yes, I should have known better. Or, maybe in the popular vernacular, I just didn't give a shit. Either way, I found my future balanced on the tip of a knife.

"Again, to keep it short, I'll only say I managed to pull the knife away before he could…well, I guess 'rip' would be the correct term…rip me open. Instead, I did something that night I swore I would not be capable of.

"Using his own blade, I opened him up, slicing a gash big enough to allow my hand to pass under his ribs and inside his body. He was still alive, and I felt the beating of his heart, rapid, scared, unused to this type of violation being turned on him.

"I ripped his heart out of his chest. And, in the valise that I'd taken to carrying with me, I took out the still-beating heart of the one that I had loved, and I pushed it into the opening I had made, pushing it into the space that I'd recently created.

"I *felt* it as it settled into its new home. I had only intended to rid myself of this burden, leaving the body to be found and me to be rid of this blessing that was swiftly becoming a curse.

"Instead, I felt as the heart took root. Then I felt the wound tightening around my wrist, and yanked my hand back. Within a moment, my former attacker, drenched with his own blood, stood and looked at me, the wound now fully closed.

"He raised his booted foot and crushed the old heart flat.

"He then called me by name.

"And god help me, he told me he loved me."

♦♦♦

WHAT THE HELL?

But the weird thing is, what you describe hits home with me. You say he wants to kill you, and boom, he's professing his love to you?

Aside from the wanting to kill you part, it's damn familiar.

Just like me. I'd been living my life, then it was like I was suddenly aware of you in the world, and nothing else mattered.

Only you.

"AS MUCH AS I hadn't planned for this, I realised that perhaps this is what had been missing. There comes a time when the loneliness is too much to bear. A companion seemed to fill that yawning, empty space. And, who would be more suitable for a never-aging woman with a dark secret than a man who both had secrets of his own, and now carried my own secret in his chest?

"Life became good again. We travelled, him and I.

"The predilections that had driven him until the moment we met seemed to have been crushed much like his old heart had been. And for a time, we had a good life. Until we didn't.

"Perhaps, losing my husband so young, and walking away from my children changed me. Perhaps it was being on my own too long that changed me. I'd enjoyed his company, then, for whatever reason, I found I no longer did.

"I'd hoped I could make him leave, but he swore—much like you—that he would never leave me.

"Instead, I left him, and I had to take the heart back to do it."

NOW YOU'RE TRULY creeping me out.

You peel off the wall, and you approach me. You reach out your hands and the reaction is automatic, somehow overriding my concerns…I reach out my own. The touch of your skin on mine feels like home.

Until you clench your fingers tight.

"AFTER HIM, I decided I was done. I knew I could not be rid of the heart in other ways, so I had one last gambit to try. After I took the heart back, it took almost fifty years to find my opportunity.

FIFTY YEARS?

♦ ♦ ♦

"YOU REMEMBER YOUR car accident two years ago, Libi? Of course you do. I was driving not far behind you and watched your car leave the road. I knew I would never have a better opportunity.

"I pulled off, climbed down the ravine and found you, thrown clear through the front windshield. You were so broken, Libi. I didn't even need to cut you. I just reached into your dead body and pulled your heart out. It was still warm, but not beating, and I remember thinking, *how unusual to not feel a heart beat in my hand now.* Incredible how the miraculous can become so commonplace when you live with it for so long.

"Having disposed of the heart in your corpse, I left.

"Imagine my surprise when you showed up on my doorstep three months later.

"I WASN'T DEAD," I say. And, "Fifty years? How old are you?"

You say, "you wouldn't believe me if I told you."

"Because the rest of this is so believable."

"*Touché,*" you say. Then, you tighten your grip on my hands and smile.

"Two hundred and twenty-eight years old next month."

I can't even laugh, the number is so preposterous.

"I KEPT RUNNING from you, Libi. You kept finding me.

"And now I know there's precious little I can do to escape this heart. This curse."

♦ ♦ ♦

THE LOOK IN your eye is unreadable. I grasp your hands hard as well. I need to show you that I'm not the same as the others.

I couldn't smother you. I just need to be *with* you.

I just need to be with *you*.

"I know now what has to happen," you say. "It's the only other thing I can think of to do."

Then I feel your grip relax on my hands.

♦ ♦ ♦

MICHELLE REACHES INTO her bag, and pulls something out. It's carefully wrapped in some paper, stained dark, with words, and a dark bit of silk.

It's her knife. The one she took from Jack.

"I'm taking back my heart now, Libi."

♦ ♦ ♦

THERE'S A FLASH. It feels like you punch me, until I feel the pain that swells in after it.

The pain spirals exponentially as you open me wider. I can't move. I can only fall to my knees.

How can you do this to me?

Then I feel a strange pressure in my chest. I can't breathe. There's a wash of cold over my head and my vision narrows.

I'm blacking out.

I think, *You killed me? But I love y –*

The darkness bleeds in.

MICHELLE LETS LIBI fall the rest of the way to the ground, slumped against the brick wall.

She wraps the heart one last time in silk and poetry, and lifts the bloodied knife from beside the dead meat that was once Libi.

"I'm sorry," she says. "I didn't mean to cause you heartache."

She realizes that could be taken sarcastically, and she can only hope Libi understands it wasn't meant that way.

She looks around the alleyway. *No, this won't do.*

What she wants to do next, she can't do here.

THE BEACH IS on a small lake, not the Gulf of La Spezia where the heart was one of the few burned remains of her late husband.

No, it's not the same at all, but it would have to do.

Michelle—no, she should be Mary now, Mary Wollstonecraft Shelley—stands on the beach and looks out at the moon-dappled waters.

Why, Percy? she thinks. *If you love me, why curse me like this?*

She can only think it may be the jealousy of her success over his own.

Perhaps.

Or, perhaps it's because the heart could save everyone but him?

Perhaps.

Whatever the reason, it is time to end it.

She unwraps the beating heart for the final time. It's beating faster now, as though it's somehow aware of her intentions.

Perhaps you are.

She gets on all fours, one hand supporting her weight and also clutching the knife, point up, toward her. With her other hand, she positions the warm, beating heart between her breasts, then just to the left a bit.

Taking a deep breath, she falls, the knife piercing first the heart that's caused her so much pain, then her own.

As the blood of both hearts bleeds into the earth, she turns her head to the uncaring night sky. She can only trust that killing both hearts will stop the curse.

She longs for nothing but darkness as pervading as the distant night sky.

Peace, at last.

♦♦♦

LATER, HER EYES flutter open once again.

She's aware of the twin beats in her chest. She thinks, *damn you.*

And the answering thought…

Here we are.

STORY NOTES

THIS ONE HAD an unusual birth.

One of my favourite songs by the Bee Gees—okay it *is* my favourite song by the Bee Gees—is "Nights on Broadway." I think it may be that really cool bass line, but overall, I just love the song.

But long ago, I also realized it really is a stalker song. I mean, the singer spying on the person in a room full of strangers basically says he'll wait forever, even if the other doesn't want them to. It's creepy.

Probably another reason I love it.

Shortly after I finished *The Lineman* (that you'll find in *UGLY STORIES, VOL. 2*), I was so damn happy with how that story came out after having been based on a song, that I wondered if I could put some kind of a spin on the "Nights on Broadway" stalker.

Interesting side note here: when I started seriously getting ready to write the story, I wasn't sure exactly what direction I was going to take it in, so I thought, *why not see if I can get some inspiration from a wholly new source?* Everyone was talking about how wonderful it was that AI could write stories and books for us now.

So, I went to ChatGPT and said, "write a story based on the Bee Gees's 'Nights on Broadway'" and it spit out a three-hundredish word story in a few seconds.

Now, to be fair, yes, it had a beginning, middle, and end, it was definitely built around the lyrics of the song, and it had a main character story arc. And holy shit, was it bad. Bland as hell.

And that didn't surprise me in the least. I determined then and there that I would never trust AI for anything more than the most banal and repetitious of tasks.

I do want to be clear here, just in case: I had no intention of using any story AI generated, and not a single phrase of the AI story made it into this one. I deleted it after reading it, and actually never thought of it again until sitting down to write this. I don't like AI, I don't use AI, and I don't endorse AI.

Clear?

Good.

So, after that experiment, I still required some inspiration. I will say, I rarely seek it out. I tend to passively wait for it, because I know when I'm in sponge mode, something will always find its way to me.

And I wasn't disappointed.

Two things came in quick succession.

The first was some article that I found—then lost—that was something about a woman who's husband had passed away, donated his heart, and now the recipient, who the woman had also married, had passed away...

...or something along those lines. Honestly, it's not even important, because that little bit was enough to create my stalker. He had the donated heart.

The second thing that seemed less like inspiration and more like just a cool fact, was the rumour that Mary Shelley had kept her husband's heart wrapped in one of his poems and some silk for thirty years after he'd passed. Her children found it in one of the drawers of her desk.

Again, reality is far more boring, and experts believe it to be his liver or something. But once the rumour sunk its claws into my writer's brain...

It still took some time for the story to coalesce, but once it did—three days ago as of this writing—the story came fast.

One last thing…I'd never planned on having Mary Shelley as the main character. In fact, I actively lobbied my writer's brain to *not* do that.

Yet, there I was, three days ago, thinking I was just getting a little bit more of the story down, when Mary Wollstonecraft Shelley stamped her foot and demanded to be the murderous star of the show.

Who the hell am I to say no to Mary Shelley?

RED RAIN

"WHAT ABOUT HER?"

"No tits."

"You say no tits, I say athletic. How bout that one?" He didn't point, just a spare, economical gesture with his head.

"Too many friends."

They both considered the possibilities in silence.

Both seemed to notice her at the same time. She came out of the store from their left, carrying a big, logoed bag and her purse slung under her arm. Cut-off jean shorts, a more modest Daisy Duke, a low-cut top tight enough to accentuate her breasts without shouting about it. Minimal jewellery. Minimal make-up.

And all alone.

But there was something else about her. Not like a glow or an aura, but...something. Something that just naturally drew the eye toward her.

"Her?" he asked.

"Her," the other replied. "She's perfect."

♦ ♦ ♦

IT WAS TOO easy—ridiculously easy—to get her into the camper van. Buck expected more problems. Hell, he expected a fight, a narrow escape, mace, screaming…something.

Chippy and Turbo were the experts. They'd done this before; they were the ones responsible for picking the product and getting it back to the van. They'd both bragged about how easy it had been in the past, back when the four of them—Buck, Chippy, Turbo and Duke—had discussed it in a drunken stupor the weekend before. Buck never envisioned they'd actually go through with it.

Though, now, sitting in the tan captain's chair in the belly of the aging camper van, seeing her sitting with her back to the wall, her breathing fast and shallow, Buck couldn't help but feel a little stirring. A little excited.

It was wrong, what they were doing. It was dirty, but the thrill was undeniable.

Turbo—Brian Turbenche to anyone that didn't know him well—was up front, piloting the creaking van out of town, a ridiculously massive drive-thru cup of high-octane coffee in one hand, a cigarette pinched between two fingers, steering with his knees. His mirrored sunglasses gave away nothing whenever he glanced in the rearview at the rest of the crew. But that was vintage Turbo. Give nothing away for free when you can charge a fee.

Beside him, already working through his third Whopper of the day, Chippy's fat ass flowed over either side of his seat, his jeans straining threateningly to contain his bulk. Greg "Chippy" Baxter did a lot of pot. Chippy did a lot of everything. Excessively. The last time Buck talked to him about this, mentioning he may have addictive tendencies, Chippy just came back with, "I toke, therefore I chow down."

Yes he did.

Around a mouthful of processed shit, Chippy asked how she was doing.

Buck looked her over again. Those long long legs, tanned a nice light brown and with a teenager's effortless tone. Long brown hair, bangs currently shading her eyes a bit, but not enough that he couldn't get a solid read on them. Scared as hell. But still cautious, waiting to see what would happen.

"S'all good," Buck said. He gave her what he hoped was a hopeful, trusting smile, but she wasn't looking at him. She watched Duke's hand as it came to rest on one of those smooth brown legs. He stroked her from knee to mid-thigh and the sound was like silk.

"Yep," Duke said, his muscled and calloused hand still doing its slow slide. "It's aaallll good." His reddened eyes looked out from under heavy lids. He'd gotten into Chippy's stash as well.

The girl abruptly yanked her leg away from his touch as her mouth puckered down in disapproval. Still, she said nothing. Duke's hand floated in mid-air for a moment, like Wile E. Coyote just after he's run off the cliff, but before the drop. Then his fingers flexed and his hand retreated. He made his own disapproving face.

"Y'doan wanna be like that, honey," he said.

Honey. Buck hated that term. There's a certain intimacy to that term that he felt should only be used between two people who were in love. And then only sparingly.

Then he smiled, because if he said that out loud, any one—and more than likely all three—would call him a pussy, and he wouldn't be able to deny it. He sounded like a goddamn chick even to himself.

Still, he didn't like it. Didn't like hearing it slurring from Duke's piehole.

He leaned forward in his chair. He tried on his friendly face again. "What's your name?" he asked, his voice low and calm.

She seemed to tear her gaze away from Duke reluctantly, obviously not trusting him to touch her again, and looked at Buck. Her eyes were a deep, soulful brown, the irises overlarge and innocent, like a child's.

She was still a child. *Jesus Christ, what are we doing?*

His hands trembled briefly until he knotted them together. He didn't think anyone had noticed.

Now getting her name seemed important.

"What's your name?" he asked again.

She opened her mouth, then closed it to swallow. Buck reached into the cooler, wanting to find her a water, but finding only beer instead. Locked and loaded and ready to party. There was a case in one of the cupboards, so Buck went and opened the case, broke the seal on a bottle and handed it over to her.

Her movements tentative, she accepted the water, took a small sip, then another. Then she downed half the bottle.

"Stacy," she said. "Stace."

"Stace," Buck said. "Stace. That's a nice name." She didn't smile, but she seemed to somehow loosen a touch.

Better.

THE FIRST RAPE almost made Buck sick.

Turbo found a spot he called "far off the grid," and Buck believed him. If he had been forced to walk home, he would have no idea of which direction to start. Looking out the windows, he saw only craggy hills and reddish rock. As though Turbo had driven them to Mars.

Dry and desolate, it matched Buck's soul right then, and he remembered thinking, forgive me for what I'm about to do. All the while knowing there would be no forgiveness. None given, none to be received.

When the van stopped moving and the rumbling engine silenced, it felt like the world suddenly held its breath. The quiet felt oppressive, like a heavy damp blanket thrown over Buck when he couldn't breathe already. His skin prickled and sweat formed in the small of his back.

Around him, the other three sported too-wide grins that held no warmth, only pain and malice. Turbo rose from his seat, took a long last drag on his cigarette, then dropped the butt into the dregs of his pool of coffee. The smoke seemed to crawl out his mouth with a slow anticipation and roil around his head. He smiled.

"Well ladies," he said, his voice too loud in the crowded camper van, "let's get this motherfuckin' party started!" He and Chippy highfived each other. Duke grinned even wider. Buck painted a smile on his face, but it didn't extend to his eyes, or back into his brain.

"Chippy and I found her, so we got dibs," Turbo said. Turning to Chippy, he said, "Did you go first last time, or me?"

Chippy's brow furrowed. "You did, dude."

"Fuck you, man," Turbo said. "I'm rememberin' now and you saw the last one first and called dibs. That sweet little redhead with the tattoos. Remember?"

Chippy said no, but his smirk said he did.

Turbo didn't wait. His hands went to his belt buckle, a Harley Davidson emblem the size of a dinner plate. It swung down and wide, thunking against the cabinets. His buckle and fly undone and, hooking thumbs under his underpants, yanked the works down in one fluid motion, leaving his semi-erect cock bouncing free and obscene. A small hoop looped out from the purpled end, like a ring through a bull's nose.

A small gasp came from the girl. *Stace,* thought Buck. She pushed backward into her corner, making herself as small as possible.

"What is it, the ring?" Turbo said, pinching the ring and lifting his manhood. Buck saw the skin stretch slightly, then had to look away from it. There was no getting around it. It was kinda gross.

"You're gonna love this. This'll take you places you only dreamed of, girly." As he talked, he stroked his shaft, hand running from the base back out to the bull-ring and back again. He didn't seem to need much stimulation for the thing to stick out like a goddamn flag pole, but still he worked it. His eyes never left the girl. "Set 'er up, Chip."

Chippy jumped to obey, likely realizing the sooner Turbo was done, the sooner he'd be in there. Duke stood. "Whaddya want me to do?" he asked.

"Pull her down, then take an arm," Chippy said. Duke reached over for an ankle and Stace pulled herself into a tighter ball.

"Don't worry," Duke said. "You'll like this. Promise." His hand closed around her leg and he pulled, Chippy reaching in for the other and together they laid her out flat on the bed. Chippy said, "Buck, give a brother a hand, willya? Get the bottoms off."

Stace struggled in vain, her mouth making a small circle where tiny quiet "no's" fell out softly.

Buck stood where he was, only his eyes reacting, getting bigger. He didn't necessarily *balk* at the task, more hesitated.

"Nuh-uh," Turbo said, one hand still working himself. "That's *my* job. Buck, you just stand back and look pretty. Don't worry, you'll get summa this too."

"No, no, no, no, no, no, no, no, no, no, no, no, no, no, no, no, no."

He reached between Duke and Chippy and delicately unfastened first her belt, then the button and fly to her cutoffs. Reaching around to the back of her waist, he grabbed and pulled, not harshly, but with authority, and her shorts and underwear came down to her sunbrowned calves in one fluid motion.

Turbo laughed softly. "Almost like I done this before, huh?" Buck found he couldn't look at Chippy or Duke's ridiculously gleeful smiles. He couldn't look at Turbo without seeing that obscene piercing, and he couldn't look at Stace.

"Oh, dudes," Turbo said. "Lookit that."

They seemed to have forgotten Buck, which suited him fine. Because he found he simply could not look at Stace, or what they were about to do to her.

The crimes they were about to do.

Turbo took his turn.

Buck didn't seem to know where to look.

But he damn well knew where not to look.

AFTER THAT, IT got so much worse.

Then Chippy took his turn. And it was bad.

Then Duke took his turn. And it was bad.

Then it was Buck's turn. And he felt his gorge rising.

"COME ON, BUCKY Boy, she's all wetted up and good to go!" Chippy grinned.

"I loosened her up for ya, buddy," Duke said, clapping his hand on Buck's shoulder, and Buck could smell the sex on him, the stink of it. His adam's apple bobbed. He looked down at the girl, the tears leaking down her temples, wetting her hair, pooling in her ears. Her mouth turned down, a mouth he was sure, up to this point, had been much more used to smiling. Her breath hitching, her fingers clenched to tight fists.

"Not right now, guys, I think she could use a break." He looked at her again, painful as that was. "Don't you think she could use a break?"

"Hell no," Turbo said. "We just got her good an' broken in for you."

Chippy, Turbo and Duke looked at him expectantly. It was his turn now. He knew that. He knew there'd be questions if he didn't. Uncomfortable questions.

His hands slid to his belt buckle. Her eyes seemed to die as they bled fresh tears. Then he saw something break in Stace. His hands kept working, but as the belt swung free and his fingers went for the button of his jeans, he heard a rumbling, like thunder, like a large slumbering beast, recently awoken, and he paused.

"Whaddya waitin' for?" Duke asked, buttoning up his own jeans.

He opened the button at the top of his jeans, gripped the tab on his fly and pulled down. Then he staggered as the van was buffeted with wind that set it rocking and the keys jangling in the ignition.

He pulled his fly back up. "I think there's a storm coming. I'm going to ride it out first, before…"

"Before you ride *her* out! Ha!" Chippy said, nudging her. She didn't seem to react, just the leaking of tears. Turbo opened the cooler, pulled four beers out by their necks and tossed one to each before popping the cap on his own and with a quick, practiced motion, brought his hand up beside his head, snapped his fingers and sent the beer cap arcing into a garbage box up near the cab.

"Two points," Duke said, and they clinked bottles, just before the van rocked again.

Turbo, Chippy and Duke moved to the front of the camper, Turbo taking the driver's seat, Chippy the passenger's and Duke took the floor, his back to some cabinets. Buck seemed almost forgotten.

He knew there was only beer in the cooler, nothing else, so he bent to Stace, lifted her head slightly and lowered the bottle to her trembling lips.

"Take a drink," he said, softly.

As she did, Buck looked out the dirty window. No clouds.

THE ONE BEER turned into many, and eventually the three of them passed out.

Buck sat with Stace, not touching her, just staying beside her. It got dark, and his eyes grew heavy.

He woke to a shaking presence, and when his eyes focused and grew accustomed to the dark, he saw Stace was holding herself, arms tight across her chest, tendons tight and drawn in her neck, teeth clenched.

"Shhhhh...shhhhh..." he said, stroking her hair.

Outside, it was raining.

"WAKEY WAKEY, HANDS off snakey," Chippy said.

Buck became aware of Chippy's annoying voice the same time he realized the shaking wasn't the wind, but Duke prodding his shoulder with a beefy hand.

"What's goin' on?" Buck glanced over at Stace; her eyes were wide and flicking between the four of them.

"We had a little nap, then Duke got the beer farts and woke us back up, so we decided it was time for a pig roast," Chippy said. Buck wasn't interested in finding out if it was the sound or the smell that ultimately woke them up. He glanced at his watch.

"Jesus, guys, it's three-fucking-thirty in the morning. Can't we wait until morning?"

"Now," said Turbo. "And morning." His smile didn't reach his eyes. "C'mon, move," he said.

Buck slid off the side of the makeshift bed—actually the table dropped down to the bench seats and the cushions spread across—as Chippy and Duke got on and manhandled the girl up to her knees.

"Take all that shit off her," Turbo said, waving his hand in the direction of her clothes. "She should be naked for a pig roast."

She tried to resist, she really did, but it didn't seem to be in her. Instead, she emitted a soft mewling noise as her clothing was stripped away, and somehow, to Buck's ears, it was worse.

When Duke had her top off, he pushed her down so she was on all fours, and he went to work on his pants. Chippy did too.

"Guys?" Buck asked, "What's a pig roast? Is that a real term?"

"You betcha," Chippy said, pulling free his already thickening cock from his boxers. "Ain't you ever heard of a pig roast?"

"Obviously he hasn't," Turbo said. "Duke, educate the man."

"Well," Duke started, "you know how you put a pig on a spit to roast him, doncha?"

"Yeah."

"Well, this is the same deal." Duke pointed his index fingers at each other and poked them together. "She gets the pole from both ends, so she looks like a pig roast."

With that, Chippy smacked Stace's ass. Duke lifted his shaft to Stace's trembling mouth. He rubbed the head against her lips. "C'mon, piggy, y'know you want it." He slapped her cheek, not lightly. "Now suck it. Suck it like a good little piggy."

At the same time, Chippy was spitting into his hand and slicking the head of his cock, then wobbled forward on his knees until he was just behind her.

Once again, Buck found somewhere else to look, but he couldn't escape the grunting, the slapping, the profanities, or Stace's alternating gagging and crying.

It took far too long for the two men to finish, but finally they both did, within seconds of each other.

"Thanks for the ride, bitch," Chippy said. Duke didn't give her a second look, just tucked himself away and zipped up.

Buck noticed the rain pattering against the roof once again. Then he was drawn back to the commotion in front of him again.

Stace was sobbing, spit and worse running from her opened mouth.

"Shut the fuck up, bitch," Turbo said, "or I'll fuckin' give you something to cry about."

That threat pushed her over the edge. The screech that tore loose from Stace brought gooseflesh to Buck's arms.

"Buck, shut her up."

Buck looked at him, not clueing in.

"Put. The gitch. In. Her piehole."

"Turb—"

"Now." There was no quarter in his tone.

Buck stooped, picked up the offending underwear, wadded it to a tight ball and moved to her mouth, still bellowing.

"If you're not gonna shut up, I'm gonna stuff this in your mouth," Buck said, trying to keep the resistance from his voice. "That what you want?"

But he could see she couldn't stop. She was trying, he could tell, but she couldn't stop. He took the wadded ball and shoved it in her mouth. He had to push as she fought him, using more force than he wanted to.

The sound level was instantly dampened.

That's when Buck heard the rain scale up a notch. Then two or three more. Then the pattering turned to clattering.

"What's that? Fuckin' hail?' Duke said.

"Sounds like rocks," Chippy said, smirking.

Then a crazy-loud bang shook the camper and a hole opened in the side of the structure, maybe a little better than an inch wide. Chippy made a squeak and was silent.

"What the fuck?" Turbo said, wiping something from his face.

Chippy.

It was part of Chippy he wiped away.

Chippy still reclined on the couch, but most of his head was gone, in a direct line from the hole in side of the camper to the massive divot in the other side. A large, dripping stone sat just below the divot, its deadly energy expended. It seemed to be the same for the rain outside as well.

Turbo drew closer, trying to get a better look at the now still Chippy. He pushed Stace to the side where she fell bonelessly, unconscious.

Apparently she's expended too, Buck thought.

"Oh man, aw man," Duke said, looking at Chippy's ruined head. "What do we do now? What do we do with him?"

"What do we do with her?" Buck asked. "We're done here. It's done."

Turbo didn't seem fazed by the events, once he'd wiped the blood and muck from himself. Tossing the bloodied rag to the side, his eyes narrowed.

"Let's go outside. Grab a smoke and clear our heads."

"What about her?"

"Don't worry about her. She's down for the count. Hell, I'd lay odds she couldn't walk right now if her life depended on it."

They headed out of the camper. Buck spared a quick look back, but she didn't move.

They stepped out onto wet earth. Duke produced a pack of cigarettes and they each took one. Turbo's Harley Davidson lighter fired them up. They each took a long first drag, sucking the smoke deep into their lungs. As Turbo blew it back out, he tilted his head and looked at the camper.

"I'll be damned."

The other turned to see what he was looking at. It was the camper itself. It had been hammered and pounded. The sideview mirrors were on the ground, the glass in shards. The only thing that seemed to have saved the front windshield was the overhanging upper bunk. Stones of all sizes littered the ground.

All of which would have been weird enough. But there was still one more thing.

The rocks. They were all reddish. And coated with…what was that?

Buck squatted and picked up a dripping stone. "Blood?"

"Must have been from Chip."

"All of them?"

"No way. That one's still in the camper."

"So the alternative is…"

"…that it was raining blood and stones. That's bullshit."

"Is it?"

"Okay," Turbo said. "Enough. We gotta get rid of them and get out of here."

"And how in the hell we gonna do that," Duke asked, dropping his butt in the wet stones.

"It's simple. Knock out their teeth. Cut off their fingers. Slice off any identifying marks, like Chip's tat on his arm," he said, pointing to his own right bicep. "Hack off a few other areas to throw them off, then we dump the bodies. Then we burn the camper to the ground."

"Jesus, Turbo, that's kind of cold, ain't it?" Duke said. "Wasn't Chippy your best bud?"

"Yeah, and I don't want my next best bud to be my fuckin' cellmate. Let's git 'er done."

♦♦♦

AFTER TURBO RUMMAGED around in a storage compartment on the outside of the camper, the three of them clambered back in the camper. The air was awash with blood and sweat and shit and sex. Buck covered his gag with a cough.

Duke looked at Turbo. "Which one you wanna start with?" They all looked at the girl. Her eyes fluttered. They all shifted to what was left of Chippy.

"Take him," Turbo said. "He ain't gonna bitch if we practice on him." He tossed the tire iron. "Take that gag from her mouth, stick it in his. That way the teeth won't go down his throat."

"Shit," Duke said. "You done this before?"

Turbo said nothing, just turned for the front of the camper. He settled himself in the driver's seat, fired up the tired engine, and pulled the lever down.

"Hold on to yer diapers, kids, this show's goin' on the road."

After a quick glance at Duke, Buck pulled the rag from Stace's mouth, handed it to him. Duke stuck it in Chip's mouth. There was a smacking noise from Stace as her mouth worked, as though trying to summon some moisture back to her mouth. Her eyes clenched tight.

Duke raised the tire iron, his fist white-knuckled around it. He brought it back down in a tight, controlled arc and impacted squarely on Chippy's front teeth with the sound of popping bubble wrap, muted only by the material jammed in his mouth. There was a moment of stillness, the quiet broken only by the hum of wheels on pavement and the low growl of the engine.

Duke lifted the tire iron again. Buck noticed the rust that had transferred from the weapon to the jagged remains of Chippy's teeth. "Heh, ol' Chip's definitely living up to his nickname now, isn't he?" He was smiling far too much for Buck's liking, but he let it go. Duke was a helluva lot bigger and meaner than Buck.

Duke raised the iron to eye level. "Goddamn!" he said, eyeing the small white bits of enamel, like flakes of porcelain. Buck could see how impressed he was with the level of damage and it worried him. Would he bother to kill Stace before he did it to her, or was it the next logical evolution of damage for him?

Then he had his answer when Duke turned his attention on Stace. "Line her up, Buck, might as well keep bashing."

Buck's stomach rolled, but damn him to hell, he moved to comply.

"This is—" was all Duke got out.

Then Hell was loosed.

The car just stopped. There was no slow down, not even the rapid deceleration of a high-speed impact. No, one nanosecond the car was doing somewhere around seventy miles an hour, the next, it's stopped. The results were tremendous and immediate.

Everything inside the vehicle—with the exception of Stace and the area around her, it seemed—still had the momentum it had had when the camper was in motion, and inertial forces threw it all violently forward. And yet…

And yet, beyond all reasoning, perhaps using the same physics that protected her, the camper's windows didn't break and allowed nothing to escape. The windows didn't break, but the three men did.

Turbo was thrown viciously forward, the steering wheel driving into his chest and belly. An incredible fount of blood and internal bits spattered the inside of the windscreen.

Buck was bounced from one end of the camper to the other, actually passing over the writhing but undamaged Stace before crashing into the cabinets on the far side, cracking through the cheap paneling before coming to rest. *Fuck me, I think I dislocated my shoulder,* Buck thought.

Duke took the worst of it, soaring from the back of the camper, cracking a couple of limbs on the same cheap paneling as Buck, but mostly missing them on his way toward the front window, mere inches from Turbo's impact site. When he ultimately came to rest mostly in the space between the two front seats, he'd broken both arms, and at least one leg, judging from the jutting shards of bone. One eye no longer contained any white, only the blood red of impending doom for its carrier.

Turbo spat blood through shattered teeth—the irony not fully escaping Buck—before he finally burbled, "The fuck happened?" There was nothing in front of the camper, so it was obvious they never hit anything.

"Don't know," Buck said.

"It's her," Turbo said. "It's that fucking bitch." And Buck knew he was right. Buck knew because he could still feel himself tumbling over her, but he also knew as he had come closer to her, he'd slowed down. He knew he slowed down a bit before passing over her to hit the cupboards.

And she hadn't moved from her unprotected spot on the bed.

How does that happen?

"It's her, ain't it?" Turbo screamed. Buck heard his struggles, but he didn't seem to be able to extricate himself. Duke seemed to be coming around, God knows how.

"Buck, kill that bitch. You gotta kill her."

Buck crawled to the end of the mattress, pulled himself up. She writhed, sweating, eyes clenched tight, blood streaming from the atrocities they'd visited upon her.

"Kill...bitch."

Buck ignored Turbo, the thought not even forming in his head. He was more interested in getting closer to her, just to touch her, to understand her in some way.

But he couldn't. He couldn't get to her. She was cocooned. It felt to Buck like the air was somehow denser around her. Soft, pillowy, yet unyielding. He pushed harder, then stopped as a noise startled him.

It came from everywhere in the camper at once. Not loud, just a jumble of clicks, clinks and taps, all occurring only once, and all at the same time.

As he searched for the source of the sound, it became obvious.

All the items in the van rose to waist height and, to Buck's mind, as fast as the camper had gone from movement to still, these shot from stillness to movement. As before, no sense of lead-up. They were motionless in the air, then they go. Each item on its own trajectory, each item—wrappers, bags, bottles, teeth, caps, screws, change, keys, dust, leaves, chips of wood, Formica, plastic—each one a bullet.

The three men, even limited as they were by their injuries, still pawed and dug in a panicked, futile attempt to open door handles, break windows red tinted by the blood rain now streaming down their outsides as though in sympathy for the red rain occurring inside.

Fabric and vinyl and skin tore under the onslaught.

Metal and windows and bone were scoured and gouged.

Howls and wails and pleas went on and on far longer than they seemingly should have been able to. Longer than lungs should have had the capacity. Longer than would be necessary to break anyone down, physically or mentally.

Outside, night turned to dawn, turned to day.

Inside, the screams went on.

Then, suddenly as it began, it ended. The rain, the projectiles, the now-guttural moans. All of it.

Gone.

Inside the camper, only blood remained.

Blood slicked over every surface, small lumps and gobbets of gore stuck to all surfaces.

Everywhere except her.

Her and him.

HE SITS NOW, hunkered down in a ball, undamaged arms wrapped around his undamaged head.

Her fists slowly unclench, showing deep-arced grooves where her broken fingernails tore through the skin. Her eyes open, revealing very little white amongst the webbing of broken blood vessels. Twin tracks of blood tears run down each cheek. Slowly, all her muscles relax with infinite patience and care.

An unending time later, she rises from her pallet, her home for the last—what? Day? Two days? She winces from the violences performed on her. Her hair, stringy with oil and sweat, hangs limp in her eyes. She moves carefully, testing the limits of her injuries as she makes her way over the gore-streaked floor to his hunched figure.

Buck starts when she touches him lightly on his arm, but his head comes up and his eyes, red and swollen from crying, meet hers.

"You helped me," she says.

"Yes," he says.

"You were nice to me."

"I tried to be."

"Why did they do it?"

"I don't know."

"Why didn't you stop them?"

"I wanted to...I did."

"But you didn't."

"No."

"No."

She rises, moves to the nearest door, reaches out and grasps the scoured handle and opens the door easily. It grinds a little, as though there were sand in the hinges, and she steps out of the camper and walks away from it.

She hears him moving in there. Her hand clenches, her fingernails finding the grooved wounds yet again, and drawing fresh blood.

And the camper crushes flat on the pavement, spraying more liquid contents in freshets from any available hole.

"You didn't help me."

She turns back to the highway, walking slowly, within the bounds of her injuries.

STORY NOTES

EVEN AS I write this, I'm still very much on the fence about whether to include this mean little story. And, a month after writing that first line, as I come back to edit, and remove all of the explicit material, I'm still not sure.

If I do, it's only because it is—aside from being a horrible story—also a weird conversation piece in that it was originally written as a sort of sequel to the third novel in my *Aphotic* series, *BLOOD LOSS*.

Because the Stace character in the story was originally written as a grown up version of the precocious little girl Sam who ultimately finished things off in *BLOOD LOSS*. So, originally, the Book was going to make an appearance here too, when she called it to her.

But ultimately, I decided to go a slightly different path. Why?

Primarily because, out of all the characters I created across six books, Sam was—and always will be—my favourite, and she doesn't deserve this fate. No one does.

That being said, I believe, in total, I've written about sexual assault six times, if I remember correctly. Three of those have seen print. One is in these collections. Not sure about this one. And the sixth? I sincerely doubt the sixth will ever see the light of day.

Still, five. That's a lot, especially when Tobin the reader truly dislikes reading about that topic in his fiction.

So why the hell does Tobin the writer keep coming back to it?

Because I know many—far too many—people who have had to live that experience. Often more than one time. Usually at the hands of a loved one.

Because I think the act is one of the most despicable, evil things one person can do to another. I could explain that more, but do I really need to?

This, to me, is the worst horror.

And I'm—for better or worse—a horror author.

Yet, I will state that, every time I've called upon myself to write about sexual assault in any form, I honestly feel sick as I write it. It's fucking awful.

I've said this in interviews before, but I'll state it here for the record: When asked the very common and frequently asked question, "Why do you write horror?" my response typically goes something along the lines of…

"I write horror to take control of the demons." We all have demons, every one of us. Some have conquered theirs, many have not. I'm likely somewhere in the middle, but when I write about the horrors that we do to each other, it allows me to have some control of the particular demon. I can pull it out into the light. I can move it across the chess board in my own way. And, I can let it win if it suits my purpose, or I can crush it.

I'm gonna give you, the reader, a spoiler alert right here and now…this particular demon? Whoever perpetuates this act in a story I write?

Yeah, they're never going to fare well toward the end.

I have no sympathy for anyone who does this to another human being.

And now?

Now I don't want to talk about this anymore, because, just like every time I write a scene with this…

I'm angry.

AWAKEN THE DREAMER

SKIP TRACER WINS COURT BATTLE AFTER THREE-YEAR FEUD WITH THE LEMA'S BOBBY FLYNT

IT'S THE MOST FAMOUS FEUD IN rock music. No, not a punch up between Glenn Frey and Don Felder of the Eagles. Not even a knock-down, drag-out between Liam and Noel Gallagher of Oasis.

No, it's the ongoing feud between The Lema guitarist Bobby "Skint" Flynt and his neighbour, multi-platinum pop singer Skip Tracer.

The pair have fallen out over Tracer's ongoing plans to renovate his home. Flynt has repeatedly complained about the works, and the feud has gotten ugly in recent years, with Tracer publicly insulting Flynt on stage and in interviews. And now the feud has reignited over Tracer's latest plan to add a massive pool.

Tracer, the "You Gonna Put That In Your Mouth" star, has won a three-year legal battle over plans for the pool and other additions at his California home, despite his neighbour Flynt's objections.

The Lema legend claimed that the construction work on the pool could be "catastrophic" for his mansion.

However, as of today, Tracer's plans have now been granted council approval.

For those keeping score, it's Skip Tracer 1, Skint Flynt 0.

♦ ♦ ♦

CALLIOPE SAT IN the sub-basement apartment, reading some Aleister Crowley and quietly chuckling to herself, when a rhythmic thudding shook the rooms hard enough to make a small, crudely-carved statue of Abholos topple from its shelf and shatter on the floor.

Initially, she was more irked at the loss of the statue. Yes, in the grand scheme of things, Abholos was the boring offspring of the Great Dreamer of R'lyeh, not much different from one of those drug-addled, eternally imprisoned kids of the Hollywood elite. So, the loss of the statue was bothersome, but it was the fact that Skint had traveled to the middle of nowhere in some far-off country—Tunisia? The old Ceylon? Who knew? —to bring it back for her after one of his world tours with the band.

Skint knew her love of anything Old Ones-related outmatched even his own prodigious appetite. He'd always been so good to her.

And that's how she knew, when she mentioned this ridiculous pounding that shook her rooms, Skint would make it right.

In the meantime, Calliope did her best to filter out the pounding, turning back to her ridiculous Crowley text, and signaling for her shoggoth to clean up the broken idol.

SKINT FLYNT, BEST known as the guitarist for the most popular band of the Seventies, The Lema, stabbed at the key on his computer. That had been a fucking perfect take, until the goddamned pounding ruined the last thirty seconds or so.

Yeah, he could fix it, but Skint was nothing if not old school. He liked a single, unbroken take.

That was gonna be impossible while all this fucking pounding was going on.

Fucking Milo.

"Motherfooker," he said, pulling the guitar from his body and hanging it on the rack. It hummed with harmonic feedback from the thudding coming through the supposedly soundproofed walls.

He stalked out of the studio with as much force and anger as he could exert through his seventy-six-year-old frame. Despite his age, and his once coal-black hair now completely white, he could still bring the thunder when he needed to.

And, obviously, today, he needed to. Someone was gonna get their ass kicked.

But maybe, he thought, *I should check in with Calli first.*

ROBERT FLYNT—SKINT to his close friends, Bobby to everyone else—met Calliope almost fifty years ago, back when The Lema was just starting to get big. They'd spent two years playing every place that had a stage in America to break the band there. Despite the posters that fucked up the spelling of the band name—everything from "The Limas" to "The Lemurs," with all the possible variations that could be thought of in between—finally the States, then the rest of the world, began to buy into the swampy, thick blues rock Skint and the rest of the band were peddling.

The night he met Calli, the band—Bobby Flynt, Dave Skinner, Bill Higgins, and Bill Williamson, better known as Skint, Skinny, Higgy, and Boomer—had landed in Seattle and had booked two nights at the Edgewater. Skint could never decide if its fame or its infamy preceded it, but The Who and The Stones had both made the place an essential stop, so it was good enough for The Lema.

Where else could a guest borrow a couple of fishing rods and drop a line off their balcony?

It was early into the Seventies, The Lema on their first proper stadium tour of America, when she walked into the middle of the debauchery at the Edgewater, and into Skint's life.

CALLIOPE'S KIN WERE originally from Innsmouth, Massachusetts, but there was a period in the late 1800s when things were getting a little crazy there, so her family fled to an entirely different state, somehow ending up in Perdido, Alabama. While the saltwater of the Atlantic had always sustained their kind, it was the muddy flowing Perdido river that seemed to change them for the better.

Freshwater instead of salt. Who would have suspected?

They were able to adapt—her sister Elinor most of all, becoming one of the famed and prosperous Caskey clan—and blend into society with greater ease.

Calliope stayed more to the shadows with the turn of the century. Her sister went off to find fortune when the Perdido flooded the town in 1919. When it did so for the second time in the 1960s, destroying first the levee that had been built, and then the town itself, Elinor disappeared. Calliope also got the itch to move on, and decided it was time to visit another coast. Her skin itched to cast off the mud of the Perdido and feel the salt of another ocean bathe her clean.

She hitchhiked out to California, looking like so many other of America's disaffected youth following in Kerouac's spiritual footsteps to get on the road and find themselves.

She'd only wanted to find the Pacific. That had been her only goal.

She took her time, choosing her traveling companions carefully, looking for those with many miles to go before they sleep, and few questions for those willing to accompany them. She learned to avoid the LSD—she couldn't trust herself not to revert to her water form—and partake sparingly of the weed, which calmed her but did little else.

In between traveling, she would find odd jobs, mostly waitressing and housekeeping, to keep her in cash. It helped that she could come across as dependable, educated, and cultured when she needed to. Her sister had trained her well.

She had found California. And, despite the ocean, had not found the state to her liking.

In the early days of the 1970s, she found herself heading northward, bound for Canada.

Instead, she found Seattle. She found a group of roadies.

And then she found Robert Flynt, leader of a band named after the ridiculous religion of the even more ridiculous Aleister Crowley.

She didn't like Crowley, but Flynt was a different story altogether.

Calliope could work with Skint.

"CALLI BABY," SKINT said as he entered her rooms. He was always careful to let her know he was coming.

Skint could never be described as a close-minded man, but there'd been a couple of times he'd made the mistake of not announcing himself and he'd seen things...holy hell, had he seen things.

The first time, he'd walked in on her when she was eating, and he simply passed out. It took two days of Calli's caring and nursing for him to come back to consciousness, but it took two more weeks before he could even speak again.

The second time, he truly had no idea *what* he'd walked in on. But he'd immediately turned around, went back upstairs and attempted to kill himself. Four times. Calli and that damnable shoggoth had kept constant vigil and always ensured his attempts were unsuccessful. It took him almost three years to get right, that time.

It took him an additional two years to manage any sort of decent erection again. He never did ask her what she'd been doing. He couldn't bear to even hold the thought in his mind long enough to ask the question.

And really, he didn't want to know the answer.

In both cases, it had taken a staggering amount of drugs and alcohol before he'd been able to, if not erase the images in his mind, to at least find a way to lock them away. They rattled at the box occasionally, and threatened to wrap their feathered tentacles around his mind again, but he somehow managed to keep a lid on them.

Needless to say, there would never be a third time. He was very careful to call her name first, and not proceed any further until she responded.

"Hello, Skint."

"Are you decent?"

Her laugh was musical. "Never! Come in, darling."

Skint stepped over the threshold into her living area. She'd been living with him since the Lema days in the Seventies, but when he'd had this mini-palace built in California, he'd offered to create a separate apartment for her. It had been a decade at that point since the sex had stopped being a regular occurrence. And with him now in his seventies, and Calliope still looking exactly as she had the first time he'd seen her in that room at the Edgewater…

He simply didn't have the stamina to keep up with her anymore.

And that last accidental walk-in hadn't done much for his sex drive, either.

Still, there were occasions when the challenge was proffered, he found himself rising to it. Occasionally with some chemical assistance.

She was in her favourite chair, legs tucked up under her, a glass of wine in her hand. A book had been discarded on the ornate table beside her.

"Bobby," she said, a note of concern threading her tone, "you look vexed."

She always had the exact right word at the tip of her tongue. *Vexed. Yes, that's exactly what I am,* he thought.

"It's the construction, isn't it?" she said. "Milo's project?"

Fucking Milo.

"It is," he said. "That fookin' poof—"

"Bobby," she said, "you've been cautioned about using language like that." By Calli. By Higgy, who's daughter was gay, by his agent, by his publicist who was gay, and by multiple others.

"Sorry, Calli, but anyone who has a name like Milo Tracey—"

"I think you're well aware of how powerful certain names are."

"Of course, but Milo ain't a Great Old One."

"Nor is a name indicative of sexual preference. Or even gender." She sighed. "We've *talked* about this, Bobby."

"Fooksakes, Calli," Skint said, "he calls himself fookin' 'Skip Tracer'."

"We're getting nowhere," she said. "As per usual." She set down her glass of wine, picked up a shaker, and added more sea salt to the glass. "What can I do for you, Bobby?"

"I was considering marching over there and givin' the cockwaffle a bloody piece a' my mind."

"It is rather irksome," Calli stated. "I lost the Abholos you got me back in 77."

"Fook me," Skint said, dragging his calloused fingers through his hair. "That cost a mint, and wasn't easy to get into England, let alone the States."

"If you go over, Bobby, remember your breathing, remember your words, and for all the gods' sakes, do *not* call him a poof."

He gave her a *how stupid do you think I am?* look.

"I know how you get, darling."

Okay, well, yeah, she did at that. He changed his look to bemused innocence that fooled neither of them, and headed back out.

♦ ♦ ♦

BACK IN THE day, Skint always had a friendly competition with Pete Townshend in regard to which band was louder, The Lema, or The

Who. Though he never admitted it in public, Townshend always managed to wring a few more skull-splitting decibels out of his overworked Marshalls than Skint could manage.

And yet, for all the money spent, all the thought that went into it, all the power chords hammered out, it turns out this scrawny little pop star next door beat the mother-loving shit out of both The Who's and The Lema's greatest sonic achievements with the simple, yet effective use of the loudest construction equipment known to man.

And Skint thought, *All these years later, I was right. Boomer – god rest your unquiet soul – if only you'd have agreed to use a jackhammer on stage back in 74…*

It took Skint first ringing the doorbell multiple times, then pounding his fist on the thick oak of the door, then starting to walk away before someone answered it.

A short, good-looking woman of indeterminate ancestry said, "Hello, Mr. Flynt. How may I help you?"

"Milo in?"

She made a face as though she hadn't quite made out what he'd said. Then she grimaced and dug a finger in an ear and pulled out a bright orange ear plug. "I apologize," she said, angling that ear toward Skint. "May I ask you to say that again?"

"Milo," he said, pointing to the five foot by seven foot portrait of the man on the wall just behind her. Just in case there might be any lingering confusion. "Is he in?"

"Yes, Mr. Tracer is in the study. If you would follow me, please."

She headed down the cavernous hall to his right, before angling left to a door that was actually vibrating from the bass tones rolling out behind it. She pressed a button to one side of the door, then turned back to Skint. "Just a moment, Mr. Flynt."

Skint motioned a finger at the button. "He's got a doorbell for his study?"

"No."

The study door didn't slide open so much as explosively disappear as a short, wiry, heavily-tattooed man pushed it aside. "Skint!" he yelled over the scratching and rapping of … was that Run DMC? "You hoary old bastard! How you doing?" He managed to tone down the hyper-caffeinated enthusiasm for a moment while he addressed the help. "I've got it from here, Esmerelda." Back to Skint. "You wanna beer? Something harder? Something powdered? No?" Back to Esmerelda. "All good, Ez. I release you back into the wild." He chuckled at his own joke, and the woman gave him an indulgent, if somewhat dimmed smile.

Back to Skint. "Robert fucking Skint fucking Flynt," he said. "At my very door! How the fuck are you, my man?"

"Well, Milo—"

"Skip."

"Apologies," he lied. He knew damn well how much the infamous Skip Tracer had disavowed his birth name. "I could be better, if truth be told." Then he stopped. "Could you perhaps turn that down a tich?"

Tracer cupped a hand behind his ear, dragging his head forward. Skint just pointed to the sound system and mimed twisting a knob.

"Right, right," he said ambling over and lowering it. "Sorry, man. Probably feedbacking in your hearing aids, am I right?"

Skint let that one go. "As I was saying, I'm trying to lay some tracks down for—"

"The inevitable twenty-seventh box set re-release of The Lema's dismal seven albums? Or have you dredged up some more dreadful demos and unreleased tracks? I especially loved that 'Wichita Lineman' cover."

That shut Skint up. He hated that track. It should never have seen the light of day. Was never *supposed* to have seen the light of day.

"It's a new solo album, if you must know," Skint said. "And it's difficult to complete when there's the incessant rumble of construction bleeding through."

"Come on, Bobby!" Tracer said. "Let it bleed through! Give it an industrial vibe! Give it some *balllllls*!" And then he bent his knees and thrust his hips forward and clasped his bloody nutsack with both hands.

You've got to be bleedin' kidding me.

"Listen, I know we've had our differences, but…"

"You took me to fucking *court*, Bobby!"

He really didn't like this skinny little no-talent prick calling him by his first name. Only Calli had that honor.

"Because you rebuffed all attempts at—"

"Rebuffed," Tracer said. "Good one."

"Look," Skint said, trying to steer this back to calmer waters. "I can't imagine this is conducive to your creativity either."

"You kiddin' me?" he said. He swung a tattooed arm to encompass the room. "Look around, dude!" Skint did. Album sleeves littered the floor. There were cups of half-consumed coffee balanced on every flat surface. Ashtrays in strategic positions circled the room, and at least four of them had cigarettes trailing tendrils of smoke in the air. Books, magazines, and comics were dribbled throughout the room. And five huge flatscreens ran five different news channels. Tracer drilled a finger into his temple. "You gotta bring food to the temple, my man, am I right?"

Skint, not knowing if he was serious or not, only smiled.

"Yeah, you get it, I can see you get it! We creative types, we need *confusion* to think. We need *chaos* to create." Scrubbing the checkerboarded pink and blue tufts of hair, he said, "So that shit out there? Mashed up with my brothas from anotha motha, the DMC? And all the rest? Damn man, it's a whole inspiration gumbo!"

"Okay, but sometimes you must need the quiet."

"Yeah," Tracer said. "When I'm fuckin' *dead*." Then he laughed like it was the funniest, most original joke ever uttered.

Skint thought, *Don't tempt me, Milo.*

Tracer stepped forward, placed a brotherly hand on Skint's shoulder. "Look man, I can see we're oceans apart on this, and that's okay, my dude." He released his grip and sauntered over to one of the burning butts, pinched it between two yellowed fingers, and sucked in some smoke. "So," he said, smoke roiling out of his mouth, "here's what I can offer you."

This oughta be good.

"This whole pool and tennis court thing is costing me an assload," he said. "But, it's only money, am I right?"

Skint nodded. It was only Tracer's money, yes.

"So what's another hunnerd grand to remain neighbourly. Tell you what I'm gonna do. Howzabout I tell the guys to knock off around two instead of five. Gives you, like, what? Thirty-five extra hours per week to...uh...billow forth your monstrous riffs, or whatever you do…"

Your math skills are wondrous, Skint thought. *Hope you have better people working for you than Harrison or Joel had.*

But the offer? That actually was...well, reasonable.

"Deal?"

Skint strode forward, pleased and impressed with the outcome. "It's a deal, Skip." He held out a hand to shake on it.

Tracer said, "My man!" and slapped a palm against Skint's, then took another drag on the cigarette.

"It's almost five, so we'll let them go today, but starting tomorrow, closing time is two."

"Thank you," Skint said. "I really appreciate this."

"You can find your way out?"

Skint told him he could.

And, as he exited the gaudy mansion, he smiled. *Didn't even have to call him a poof,* he thought. *Calli's gonna be proud of me.*

♦ ♦ ♦

THAT WAS TUESDAY.

On Wednesday, Skint got up at the ungodly hour of 11 a.m., and got on his stationary bike with his noise-cancelling headphones and listened to the playbacks from the last sessions. The faintest sounds of construction bled through the headphones. *Only three more hours.*

Afterward, he dragged his aching old frame into the shower, and sipped on a disgusting concoction of blended green stuff that Calli insisted was good for him.

God, I miss the days of rolling out of bed with a bottle of Chivas and a fat blunt. But now, most of his bottles contained prescription pills and vitamins, and the only thing fat was his slowly expanding middle. And the only blunt he got now was blunt commentary from Calli who, a half-century after coming into his life, looked just as young, fresh, and sexy as the day he met her.

He sighed, and headed to the studio. He wasn't going to try to do anything until after two, but he could get everything set up, maybe review some of the tracks again, make himself some notes.

It was gonna be a good day.

Hell, he thought, *if I get everything squared away, maybe I can go visit Calli.* He liked to kid himself that he could relive the 1970s for a little bit, but being in his seventies put a damper on that. But he did still have a few tricks that, should the flesh be weak but the spirit willing, he could fall back on.

Yeah, maybe him and Calli could mess up the sheets for a bit.

He whistled between sips of green shit all the way to the studio.

TWO HOURS LATER, he'd determined that, once again, the spirit was more willing to lay down tracks than get laid.

Not that he was actually getting any music made quite yet, but damn, he'd made a lot of progress on figuring out where to go. He had a yellow legal pad filled with notes of what he was going to work on when the magic hour of 2:00 p.m. struck.

Which was in three minutes.

The green shit had been consumed, and now he was sipping on his second cup of coffee as two o'clock came and went. And the distant throaty roars of construction didn't cease.

He took one more sip, checked the time, set the coffee down again, checked the time again.

2:02

"Goddammit," he said.

He put his hands on the arms of his chair, preparing to get up and go give that poofter a piece of his mind…

When the sounds stopped.

He put his elbows up on the mixing board, put his chin on his fist, and waited.

Five minutes later, still no sounds.

"Okay," he said, nodding to his reflection in the glass that separated the studio from the mixing room. "Okay, he's true to his word." And again, Skint felt a rush of pride that he'd managed to sort this out. *Probably should have done this before throwing a lawsuit at him,* he thought. Especially when Skint had lost in court. Embarrassingly so.

He grabbed his coffee and his legal pad, and headed into the studio.

Time to make some noise of my own.

♦♦♦

HE SET THE legal pad down, placed the coffee where he wouldn't spill it, and wouldn't forget it—because goddamn, he was getting bad for that lately—and reached for his favourite black Strat.

The computer was ready to go, he clicked a few buttons. The guitar, and effects pedals, and everything else he needed was set up.

He checked his notes, slung the guitar strap over his shoulder, got the most recent track running in his cans that he'd been working on, and got ready to blow.

The bridge of the song was almost done, and he was getting ready to tear into the solo when a counter melody started up, bleeding into his cans.

The fuck?

He stripped the cans off his ears, stopped the recording, unslung his Strat, and listened.

A dull, slightly arrhythmic thudding, with some weird highs over it. He could almost place it, but not quite. The soundproofing was good here, but this was an aerial aural assault that swept past defenses never built for that kind of ferocity.

He stepped out of the studio, and the sound was instantly louder. And Skint immediately recognized it. The blood rushing to his face was literally a tactile feeling.

Wichita motherfucking Lineman, Skint thought. *I'm gonna fucking murder the cockwaffle.*

GLEN CAMPBELL, MEMBER of both the legendary Beach Boys and the even more legendary Wrecking Crew, had released "Wichita Lineman" right around the time Skint was pulling the band that would eventually be known as The Lema together, and the song was ubiquitous in the months leading up to the release of The Lema's first album.

Sure, Skint and the boys noodled with the tune, fascinated by the minor chords and the almost Morse Code-like beeping. It was a fantastic little pop song. Nothing The Lema would ever have considered recording as a cover, or even busting out live, but fun to noodle with. And hearing Skinny get knotted up in the emotion of the song, and often—despite having a powerhouse voice—completely nailing the evocative sadness inherent in the lyrics.

Unfortunately, none of those good takes ever made it to tape.

Instead, in the early, heady days of the 70s, when they were at their absolute peak and could do nothing wrong, somehow, during a drunken and drug-propelled jam, the most terrible take they had ever done of the song was recorded. It ran over nine minutes, longer than their biggest hit, "Pathway To Carcosa," and included misheard lyrics, an argument between Higgy and Skint as to who should be doing the Morse Code beeps, Skinny roaring out an obvious orgasm because some groupie had given him head during an extended solo, and it ended with Boomer loudly vomiting all over his drum kit, and then saying, "Well, that made a fookin' splash, dinnit?"

It was excessive. It was awful. Yet somehow, as their first label shat out a greatest hits package to finish off their five-album contract, they'd tacked that mess on the end as a hidden track.

It became known as the "Snort Another Wichita Line, Man!" song.

Jimmy Webb, the songwriter, sued them. The Lema sued their old label. Their old label countersued everyone.

The album was pulled from the market fairly quickly, but it gained new life with the internet.

And it was the fucking bane of Skint's existence. Harlan Ellison had this whole hate riff in the middle of his *I Have No Mouth And I Must Scream* story that was the only thing Skint had found that might adequately express his utter displeasure with that track. Just swap out the term "HUMANS" for "THAT FUCKING TRACK."

And now, blasting out from massive speaker stacks pointed squarely at Skint's house, Milo was playing the full nine minutes and fourteen seconds of it at brain-liquefying volume.

On repeat.

Mother, Skint thought, *fucker.*

♦ ♦ ♦

CALLI HEARD THE distinctive ragged opening of The Lema trying to find their way into "Wichita Lineman," then Skinny's distinctive voice—easily one of the best of his generation—nailing the first line, before killing the second with the drunken "searchin' in the sun for another rodeo."

By the Great Old One, that maniac next door's looking to get himself killed.

She knew she had to get over there before Skint got it in his foolish head to finally do it.

First, she needed to find out if he already had.

She moved to the nearest wall and stretched her arms wide, flattening herself up tight against it, knees, thighs, belly, breasts, arms, hands, and forehead, maximizing the contact as much as she could. Like she was hugging it, which, in effect, she was.

She was a creature of the water, so this weird, distant offshoot of lithomancy, appealing to the rock of the building and surrounding ground, didn't come naturally to her. But years of practicing had given her a base familiarity with it.

She reached out to the stone, gave it the requisite platitudes, and, forehead tight to the wall, begged it to look upon itself to find Skint for her.

~ *The soft one you seek is here.* ~ Then the house gave her a mental picture of his location. Just coming out from the studio.

Okay. She ran to intercept him.

♦ ♦ ♦

"SKINT," SHE YELLED, running down the hall as he stormed out. He kept right on going.

"Bobby!" *Yeah, he's on a mission.* He threw the door open, and the sound magnified, dull throbs and muted notes becoming sharp cracks and bright tones. *That godsdamned song.*

Then her shoggoth was in front of him, and he pulled up short. Looking back over his shoulder at Calli, he said, "Call off your pet, Cal. I'm going, and nothing's gonna stop me."

"Bobby," she said, and put a hand on his shoulder to spin him around. She knew her shoggoth was getting antsy. It didn't like being looked at too long by humans.

"What?" he snapped, the syllable sharp enough to cut.

"Let me."

"You? Why?"

"Because I won't kill him."

"All the more reason for me—"

She placed both hands on his chest. "Let. Me."

Maybe it was the touch. Maybe it was the look in her eyes. Maybe it was her own sharp tone. Whatever it was, she felt his chest rise as he finally took a breath, closed his eyes, and sagged.

"I just want to record some music, Calli," he said, and there was a note of desperation in his voice that she thought she understood. The man was once a musical god, and he still had enough cachet to remain rock royalty until the day he died, he also knew that day was much closer than he'd like. It was tough for Calliope to wrap her head around that, because she'd spent almost fifty years with him and, despite watching him grow old, it was still something that happened to others. She had much longer on this world before she'd even begin to show any aging.

She understood his struggle, and did her best to understand his feelings, but still, he was only human, even if a once-extraordinarily talented one. And as that talent and life faded, he wanted to prove he was more than something he did fifty years ago.

Her taking on the task of talking to the odious little man next door though? Yes, that was something she could do for Skint. That was one way she could help him.

"Stay here, Bobby," she said. "I'll get it worked out." She moved closer, looking up to catch his downcast gaze. "I promise you."

He nodded. "Okay."

He turned then, to head back inside, but stopped. He pointed to Milo's house. "First things first. Get that shite shut off."

It was her turn to nod.

It really is terrible.

♦♦♦

"GIVEN UP ON dealing with me himself, has he?" Milo said in a horrible parody of Skint's distinctive British accent. "Sent the missus over to box my ears?"

At his front door, the song wasn't quite as jet-engine loud, as the speaker stacks had been surgically directed toward the studio area of Skint's home. Calli could still hear it, but she didn't have to yell.

That didn't necessarily mean she wouldn't yell. She'd have to play it by ear.

"Mr. Tracer—" she began.

"Skip."

"—I'm Calliope, and—"

"Quality handle, Calliope!"

"—I've come to ask you to shut off the system you're using to bludgeon Skint's home with."

"Ah," he said. He clasped his hands together, as if in prayer. "See. Now that's gonna be a problem, because it's part of the agreement I entered into with Bobby."

"The problem, Mr. Tracer—"

"Skip."

"—is that this aspect was never agreed upon. You agreed to stop construction at two in the afternoon. At no point did you indicate you would fill the remaining silence with songs played at apocalyptic volume."

"I didn't *not* say it."

I should go full aquatic and drown him in his own pool.

She wouldn't, of course. Chlorine made her violently ill.

So what are you going to do? She honestly didn't know. Her only goal had been to pre-empt Skint from coming over, then ending up in jail for assault or murder.

"I'm asking nicely," she said. "I'm trying to appeal to you as a musician. Skint's not asking for the construction to stop—"

"He tried. He failed."

"Only out of concern for the safety of his home. It's quite old and—"

"Just like your boyfriend. Old and craggy."

"—he was concerned for the structural integrity—"

"Integrity," Skip said, "not a word he's likely that familiar with."

And she stopped. He was only listening enough to pick out key words to mock. This would get her nowhere.

She looked at the massive portrait hanging behind him.

She flared her nostrils, taking in more information that way.

And she stared down at him. Calli wasn't a tall woman, but she was taller than Milo, even with his height-enhancing, custom-made Adidas.

"Milo," she said.

"Skip," he said. It was automatic.

"No," she said. "Milo. Milo Tracey. 'Skip Tracer' is the name of the taller, more secure man you want to be."

"What? What the fuck you talking—"

"Come on, Milo. The big portrait behind you. The big house for just you. The constant interruptions when someone speaks to you, to show them who's boss. The big speakers blasting music. Even your ridiculous shoes that add another inch-and-a-half to your diminutive...structure."

He opened his mouth to speak as he raised a finger. She swatted it away.

"You assaulted me!"

"No Milo, I came here instead of Skint to protect you from assault. Because I know you. I *see* you. You want to be the biggest, baddest shark in the ocean, but it's tough when you're born a goldfish, isn't it?"

He went to raise his finger again, but she gave him a look and he thought better of it, lowered it again.

"But it all hides something else, doesn't it, Milo?" she said. "One of the two things you have that truly are big. One is your insecurity. But the other one is...your big secret."

"You don't know me, bitch. And you sure as hell don't—"

"Want me to piss on you, Milo?"

His mouth open, closed, opened, and closed a final time. He looked like...well, yes, he looked like a goldfish.

"No," she said. "You don't. It's boys you prefer."

"How do you...?" he said, then changed tack, "You don't—"

"Oh Milo," she said, leaning in. She made a show of taking a big sniff of him. "I can smell it on you. You shower, and you use two different soaps to wash it off. You cover yourself in a fog of Axe body spray, but beneath it all, I can easily smell the particular tang of boy urine."

"You're crazy."

"I disagree," I said. "Many would think you slightly left of centre for wanting teen boys to empty their bladders on you simply because you feel you deserve it."

"You fu—"

Calli's turn to raise a finger. "Be very careful of your next choice of words, Milo," she said. "You wouldn't want to make a *big* mistake."

"You can't do nothing to me," he said. "You have zero proof." He brought his fists together, exploded his fingers out. "*Nada*."

"You underestimate the power of doctored tweets and rumour and social media attention."

His finger slowly imploded back into his fists.

"So, before it comes to that, or even to the point where Skint drags out the full weight of his Lema sound system to broadcast Wagner at you, I suggest you pull the plug and shut down your childish attempt at proving your dick is bigger. Trust me, Milo, it's not."

He wanted to bluster, she read it in his face. She sniffed again and shut it down.

"Do we understand each other?"

"Fuck you."

"I'll take that as a yes," she said.

She turned and got only a few feet away from the door when Milo said, "By the way, it's spelled with a 'W' so it's pronounced *Waaag-ner* not *Vaaahhg-ner*. Learn some history, bitch."

Amateur hour. Not even worth a response. She smirked and kept walking.

In a louder voice, he said, "Should probably tell you, though. I got the zoning approvals this morning. The pool is just the start. Going to build a tennis court and full workout complex back there. Construction could take a couple of years."

That stopped her.

She stood still for a moment, undecided on whether to re-engage or continue her exit.

"Tell that to the ancient jerk-off next door."

Walk away, Calli. She walked away.

But the music did stop.

CALLI SPENT THE night with Skint. He needed it. She needed it.

When they'd finished with their lovemaking, she left him smoking the day's last cigarette while she quickly showered. By the time she had toweled herself dry and slipped back into the silk sheets, Skint was doing his typical sprawl of the entire bed—

seriously, how could one person take up an entire king-sized bed all on his own? —so she gave him a couple of gentle prods and he shifted enough for her to settle in and snuggle in behind him. It gave her comfort to feel his warm back against her breasts, the backs of his thighs against the fronts of hers. She slid an arm around his waist and placed her hand over his heart, feeling the soft rhythm within him, the engine that drove him to create rhythms to share with the world.

Her fingers idly playing with the hair on his chest, she let her mind drift back to that ridiculous hotel on that ridiculous night half a century ago.

The Edgewater.

♦♦♦

CYNTHIA CLAIMED SHE wasn't doing plaster casts anymore because, according to her, "the scene is just bullshit now."

But when she heard The Lema were going to be at the Edgewater, she decided on "a temporary moratorium on her moratorium," gathered her casting supplies, and enlisted a few friends to help her get in to see the band. It took some bribing, and a couple of blowjobs, but they got in. The Plaster Casters were back on the job.

Calliope had no idea what she was expecting, but she wasn't expecting anything like what they walked into.

It was a party that ran most of the floor, with all the room doors thrown open, and scores of men and women, many in the colourful hippie garb of the times—lots of flared pants, platform shoes, silk scarves, and billowy shirts—but seemingly just as many in various levels of nakedness. People were fucking in the rooms, and one particularly energetic threesome was happening right in the hallway.

In one of the rooms, a shaggy, hairy beast of a man with a mouthful of nails—she later found out he was Bill "Boomer" Williamson, drummer for The Lema—was busily hammering a nail into a chair to secure it five feet up on a wall. Most of the rest of the furniture had been similarly secured to the walls and ceiling. Cynthia angled in to that room, already prepping her speech to get him to allow her to cast his penis. Calli furrowed her eyebrows and carried on.

Most of the energy came from one room. Two men—she quickly found out they were Dave Skinner and Bobby Flynt, or Skinny and Skint, the singer and guitarist for The Lema—were holding court. There were at least twenty people in the room, and most were women.

Calli eased into the room, accepted a joint, and leaned back to watch.

It didn't take long to see who the ringmaster was—bare-chested, lion-maned Skinny—but also who owned this circus. And that was Skint. He was quieter than his partner, letting Skinny take the lead, but every so often, Skint would drop a few words, an observation here, a suggestion there, and everyone, Skinny included, would move to do his bidding.

It was Skint who ran this show.

He was intriguing. Intriguing in a way no other human had been to Calliope up to now.

Therefore, it was Skint she needed to get to know.

But how? In a room full of beautiful, adoring women and men, what could she do to catch his eye?

When Skinny pulled a small spiny dogfish out of a massive metal tub, and said, "'Oo wants to 'ave some fun, then?" she knew she found her way in.

THE EVENTS THAT transpired over the next hour have, in the intervening years, gained a level of mythology that Calli could never have expected or predicted.

But while she had prepared herself for a level of debauchery she had not yet experienced—she knew Skinny intended on using the live shark as a dildo on her—she was more distressed when, after she agreed, he pulled out a machete and hacked the poor thing's fins off to "make it more aerodynamic, yeh?"

Surprising even herself, she insisted on three things as she pulled her sundress over her head.

First, she wanted Skint to do the honours.

Second, she wanted the hacked off pieces inserted in her.

Finally, she wanted the dying fish inside her too.

Then she cleared all the people and their shit off the bed, laid down, and spread her legs.

SKINT WAS TENTATIVE at first, and she had to guide him and help him, her hands over his.

Nine minutes in, Skint's eyes widened when she flexed and the entire fish was pulled inside her. Ten minutes in, she had her first orgasm of the night, and the spiny dogfish came back out of her, head first.

Fully intact.

Still shaking and contracting from the orgasm, she grabbed Skint's wrist and panted out her demand that he throw the fish back into the water. He didn't hesitate. He carried the wriggling thing out to the balcony then, with a disbelieving shake of his head, dropped it into the Pacific.

But Skinny, witnessing this, had already pulled two more fish out and hacked at them. "Un-fookin'-be-*leev*-able. Fookin' do it agin!"

Calli caught Skint's wrist again, and stared into his eyes. He stared back only a moment.

"All right, folks," he commanded. "Show's over. Everyone out. Go make sure Boomer hasn't nailed his own dick to the ceiling."

When everyone cleared the room, she told him they had to fix the other two fish that Skinny had mutilated.

Calli got up from the bed and walked out to the balcony, still naked. Then she looked back over one shoulder at Skint.

She remembered bending and clutching the balcony guardrail, Skint first pushing the fish inside her then, as she'd directed him to do, changing position and taking her from behind. She remembered the squall of her clenching, shaking release and, in her throes, orgasming out two whole live fish in succession, back into the water.

And Skint saying, "Jesus Christ, girl. What *are* you?"

Gasping and sweating, she turned to him, draped both hands over his shoulders, and said, "I'm many things, but right now there's one thing that's very obvious."

"And what's that?"

"I'm going to be your muse."

She hadn't been wrong.

Over the next fifty years, he'd learn a lot more about the many things she was—and she about him—and his fascination never waned.

SKINT'S BREATHING HAD slowed and deepened as her fingers swirled in his chest hair. She kissed his bare shoulder.

He'd given her a good life. He was her benefactor, building her this apartment and keeping her happy for fifty years. She, in return, was his muse, inspiring some of The Lema's best loved songs.

"Battle of Pelennor Fields"

"Middle Earth Hop"

"When The Levee Breaks (Song for Elinor)"

"When Cthulhu Wakes"

"No Mercy (The Old Ones Return)"

"Inchin' Toward Innsmouth"

And of course, the big one. "Pathway to Carcosa." That eight-minute epic from the fourth album was the first one she inspired, coming only days after the Edgewater thing, and cemented the band's place in history, and cemented her relationship with Skint.

She knew the other guys didn't really get it, and once Boomer died, seemed confused that Skint had walked away from The Lema, but kept her by his side. The term "Yoko" was tossed around a lot.

They both ignored it and carried on.

Fuck them, she thought. *No one else ever took the time to know me like Skint.*

She settled herself a little more comfortably to allow sleep to come.

She was just drifting off herself when Skint experienced a myoclonic jerk, that full-body twitch that came when the body was almost asleep.

And it tweaked something in Calli's head, but she lost it as she fell into her own slumber.

THE NEXT DAY, their neighbour's construction was back up and running.

Milo also seemed to double down on the pain and torture. The workers all had ear protection on, and the speakers continued to blast a continuous loop of "Snort Another Wichita Line, Man!"

Something had to be done. He was becoming a bigger and bigger jerk by the day.

Jerk.

She'd been thinking something about that recently. What was it? Something someone had said? Skint?

No.

Milo.

Tell that to the ancient jerk-off next door.

Jerk-off.

Jerk.

Jerk. She was missing something.

And then, she had it.

She knew what she could do.

IT TOOK SOME persuading—convincing Skint to not kill Milo—some short-term solutions—lodging a noise complaint with the cops, and outfitting everyone with ear protection—and then she settled down to do some research with some very old books.

When she could only find hints of what she wanted, she knew she had to go deeper, which was a pain in the ass.

There was a time when she could have booked a flight and visited the resources in Arkham. The Miskatonic University had a fantastic selection of rare books, but with all the incidents that have occurred over the years, it had become a painstakingly long and involved and usually fruitless process to even get a look at them, let alone spend some time with them.

Gone were the days of just going in and asking to see a book that was the literary equivalent of a nuclear arsenal. It took them far longer than it should have to figure it out, but they had.

But somehow, over the years, some enterprising individuals—what they lacked in morals and intelligence, they more than made up for in subterfuge and computer ability—had managed to get parts of various books uploaded to websites that were as removed from most of the world as Kadath was from all but the most persistent dreamers.

None of the books were complete, unfortunately, because some pages simply couldn't be reproduced, or steadfastly refused to do so. Some may have been successfully reproduced, but never made it to the dark web because the imagery drove the person insane.

But Calli was no layman, no amateur. She was adept at ferreting out subtext from a few cryptic lines of text. She could catch the most subtle of references, then run them down in other tomes.

But before she did that, she had to get the staff to clear all the food out of Skint's walk-in freezer because, with what she had to do, everything would spoil. She then set up her computer in there. She had to cast protection spells first around the home, then around the freezer, then around herself, and finally around the computer. The freezer was necessary, because, despite protection, the device would become hot enough that the plastic casing would become soft. The screen sometimes needed to be coerced to display what she needed, as though the unthinking machine still had a built-in reticence to offer up some of the things she demanded.

After the set up, and the protection, it took her two days to even find the references she needed. Then another day to ensure she was indeed on the right track.

Two more days gave her the plan.

She had to borrow some shoggoths from one of Skint's rockstar friends—not that he'd miss them, he had a stable of them—to begin weaving the bubble.

With all that settled, it was time to let Skint know what was going on.

♦♦♦

SKINT WAS IN his studio. He'd been busy.

The studio was the cleanest she'd ever seen it, with all the guitars set up on stands, each one gleaming. All the keyboards and the drumkit behind its baffles were sparkling. Microphones were set up, or neatly situated off to the side for easy retrieval, and all cords were coiled and neatly stored. The floor had even been cleaned.

Skint was off to one side, performing surgery on a guitar. He was always looking for that particular tone, that sound that no one had yet made. A fat blunt sat smoking in an ashtray close at hand.

Ah, that explains it, she thought. *He got himself baked to ride out Milo's bullshit.*

He looked up when Calli entered, "Hello, my love."

"Hey baby." She didn't ask what he was doing specifically, because she knew he'd get into technical stuff that would fly over her head. Instead, she said, "Are you too busy to help me with something?"

"Never," he said, and when he smiled, she saw that sparkle in his eyes that took her back fifty years. He was very much a young man in a body aging too fast. "What can I do you for?"

"I think I may have a solution to our friend next door."

"He's no bleedin' friend of mine, Cal."

"Nor me," she agreed.

"Fair enough," he said. "What can I do to help?"

"I need some music."

"Easy enough. I've got lots stored on—"

"No," she said. "Sorry, I'm being vague, and I don't mean to be. I need you to learn a new song. Well, almost more of a suite."

"Like some classical guitar stuff?"

"Not really."

Skint was used to her oddities. Years ago, he would have dug and probed and questioned and had her explain. Now, he just said, "Okay, carry on."

"There's certain...not sure of the words here, Skint...maybe phrasing? ...certain phrasings, certain collections of notes, both together or in sequence, certain ways they must be played, how fast they come, how long they stay for… Does any of this make sense?"

He smiled again, took a hit from the blunt, nodded. The fragrant smoke curled over his lips as he said, "Perfect sense. If I can deal with Higgy's OCD technical perfection, I think I can handle this."

Calli let out a sigh of relief. "Okay, good." Then she put a hand on his knee. "But it's going to have to be done fairly quickly." She tapped her wrist. "We're on the clock here."

"Challenge accepted, love," he rasped. The smoke always brought a bit of an edge to his voice that she found endearing. "Just one thing."

"What's that?"

"You aren't going to ask me to sing, are you? Cuz you know my voice is shite."

She smiled. "No singing. Just doing what you do best, Skint. Wringing every note out until you make it bleed."

"Well that's all right then, innit? When do we start?"

"As soon as you give me a hit off that joint you're bogarting."

He handed it across and they both laughed, her sweet high tone a counterpoint to his low dirty rasp. They had always complemented each other. Calli as muse and Skint as the one that made magic out of nothing but sound.

Now, they had to do it one more time.

♦♦♦

FIVE DAYS.

For five days, they lived in Skint's studio, working up the structure of the piece—with the many changes in tempo and moods, it could hardly be called a song, more of a series of movements—from Calli's vague descriptions and Skint's translation of Calli's instruction into a story.

"It's a little claustrophobic here, can you breathe a bit of light into it?"

"I hear the blues and greens, but it needs a slash of bright red running through it. It needs to bleed."

"This part isn't pointed enough to break through barriers. Can you put a sharper edge on it, Skint?"

For five days, they'd talked, they'd fought, they'd gone off to their respective corners, they'd scribbled notes and plucked strings and plinked keys. They'd taken breaks only for the odd bite of ordered in food, to smoke, or to fuck.

Five days.

It was far too long. An eternity.

And yet, it flew by, ephemeral as a stray thought.

At the end of it, they were out of time, and Calli wasn't sure it was ready.

Fuck it, she thought. *It has to be.*

♦♦♦

"WHAT NOW, LOVE?" Skint said, scrubbing at his grey mane with a towel. They'd finished the piece—and despite five days of trying, couldn't come up with a proper title for the damn thing—and grabbed a couple hours of sleep and showers.

Calli checked the work of her shoggoths and was happy with what she saw. Shoggoths weren't the smartest or the fastest of creatures, but give them a task and some time, and they'd always do it well.

From her spot on Skint's massive Alaskan King bed, she regarded her friend and lover. He'd walked from the bathroom naked, and his hair was a fluffy white cloud around his head. His body was facing the inevitable sag of decades of gravity and slowly loosening muscle and tendon. He was still lean, and looked good for his age, but still...the years had ravaged his once-perfect body.

She looked at his hands. His finger pads were flattened and tough from years of guitar work. The tendons stood out sharply on his hands, his wrists, his forearms.

Whatever else time had taken away from Skint, it had not taken his talent or his ability. He was still one of the finest musicians of his age.

And what he'd accomplished over the past five days was nothing short of a miracle.

But would it be miracle enough?

"What now?" she said. "Now we wait for nightfall, and we sleep."

His low rasping laugh chuckled around the room. "And then what?"

"And then I take you on a dream-quest."

"To Kadath?"

She got up from the bed, walked across the room to him, laid a gentle hand on his cheek. "No, baby, not Kadath. Someplace a lot more wondrous."

As she said this, her other hand was already busy with another part of him.

If we don't make it, I want one last memory of him inside me.

"I'VE NEVER UNDERSTOOD the whole 'dead Cthulhu lies dreaming' thing. How can he be dead *and* dreaming?"

"You don't understand it, because you see death as an absolute, Skint. You're dead or you're alive. No in between."

"Exactly."

"Exactly wrong," she said. "There are shades of death. Degrees of death."

Skint cocked his head.

"Zombies are dead, but still walk. Vampires are not dead, yet not alive."

"And they're utter bollocks."

"They are both very much in this world, and—" she held up a hand to hold his questions off "—a topic for another day. There are other examples. Didn't your Jesus die and then come back a few days later?"

"I suppose, but I don't much buy into him, either."

"How about that pesky cat of Schrödinger? The one that's both dead *and* alive?"

"Yeah, sorry, love," he said, "zombie pussy weirds me out, y'know?"

"Zombie pussy...Jesus, it's not horror, Skint, it's quantum mechanics."

"Is that part of that string fookery?"

"String theory," she said.

"Yeah, that. String fookery. Because I learned long ago, any pussy with a string is just gonna end in blood and tears." He held out placating palms. "No offense, baby."

"None taken," she said.

"Anyways," he said. "It's all just zombie pussy bollocks."

Calli sighed heavily. "There's one thing you do believe in," she said. "It's another form of death. *La petite mort.* The little death. You die just a little when you orgasm. It's why some people court death while achieving sexual gratification. The closer to death you get, the better the orgasm."

"And Christ knows, you and I," he said, "we've died many times, then, love."

She smirked. "Yes we have."

"But that other stuff? Still think it's bollocks."

"Regardless," she said. "All you need to know for today is, death is not absolute. Let's leave it there."

"HOW'S THIS GONNA work, Calli?" Skint and Calli were in her bed this time.

She knew damned well how it *wasn't* going to work. No tripping down seventy steps to the cavern of flame, because trying to get those pricks Nasht and Kaman-Thah to do anything for her would be pointless. All they were interested in was oiling their shitty beards and saying no to everyone.

Tweedledum and Tweedledummer, those two are.

"We've got to do a little sneaking past a couple of priests, so we're going to sidestep the normal path down to the Gate of Deeper Slumber. Instead, I'll find you in the dream world and we'll just skip out of here, go down to the beach, and dive into the ocean."

"I'm not much of a swimmer." Skint had an Olympic-sized pool that he had never used. And the closest he'd come to the ocean was dipping his toes in the sand on the beach.

"You won't have to swim, baby," she said. "I promise."

She opened the top drawer of her nightstand, and pulled out a perfectly rolled joint. "We're going to smoke this. Then we're going to screw like stoned rabbits. Then we're going to go to sleep. And then we're going to take care of our little Milo issue."

She fired up the joint, took a long pull, and passed it over. "I think I can handle all of that," Skint said.

I hope so, she thought. *Because that last part is going to be tricky.*

"THIS IS SOME freaky shit, Calli," Skint said. He wasn't talking so much as they were sharing thoughts. Even in a dream state, it was really hard to converse when you were hundreds of feet below the ocean's surface. "Ringo was wrong."

She didn't respond in words, so much as a mental picture of a question mark.

"I don't see no fookin' octopus' gardens down here."

A purely mental bout of laughter is a strange and wonderful thing to experience. She felt Skint relax, just a little.

"Where we headed?"

"It's quite close to a spot in the ocean known as Point Nemo. It's part homage to Captain Nemo, and also aptly named because 'nemo' in Latin means 'no man'. It's literally the farthest place—something like 1700 miles—from land in any direction."

"And why are we going to such a rockin' party spot?"

"About thirty years ago, a sound—creatively named 'the Bloop'—was heard relatively near this spot. They thought it was some unknown sea monster, until it was eventually put down to a cracking iceberg."

"Let me guess...it *was* a sea monster?"

"Close. It was Cthulhu."

"Oh," Skint said. "Shit."

"And that's where we're going. R'lyeh."

"Oh," Skint said. "Double shit."

AND THEN THEY were in the aptly named nightmare corpse-city of R'lyeh, where the dead Cthulhu waited, dreaming.

"Jesu—"

"*No!*" Calli shot back. "You speak no names of any exalted ones, real or imagined in this place. You have no idea what can be unleashed."

"Right," he said. "Got it." She easily picked up the staticky panic flowing from him. She didn't blame him. The place truly was a nightmare.

Gustaf Johansen had said it best when he described the place as "mingled mud, ooze, and weedy Cyclopean masonry which can be nothing less than the tangible substance of Earth's supreme terror...loathsomely redolent of spheres and dimensions apart from ours."

The tangible substance of Earth's supreme terror. The only thing was, had he been describing Cthulhu as the supreme terror, or that the slimy, weed-choked architecture, with its brain-cracking impossible angles, immense walls, and aura of barely-shackled evil? Which was the terror of the Earth in tangible form?

As far as Calli was concerned, both were accurate.

"We're here to do one thing, Skint, then we're gone."

"What's that, exactly?"

"You're going to play your new piece for the Great Old One."

"HOW THE HELL am I gonna do that, Calli?"

"I believe I can assist in that regard."

Skint spun around to meet the new speaker. "Who the fookin'—"

"Manners, Skint," Calli said. "Erich Zann, this is Robert Flynt. Bobby, this is Erich Zann."

"A pleasure, Herr Flynt," Zann said, the words coming out as *pleh-juuuure* and *flinkt*. "Please, forgive my appearance."

Skint was staring at a short man, his hand extended. He was flanked by two cases, obviously holding musical instruments, one smaller, one much larger. Zann's skin was mouldering and chunks had fallen away, leaving yellowed bone to peek out. When he spoke, his tongue seemed to rattle about in his mouth, as though it wasn't attached and only loosely made the correct sounds. He reluctantly shook the proffered hand. "Mr. Zann." Then he tried his best to be circumspect as he wiped his hand on his pants. It was a dream world, but it was still gross.

"*Herr* Zann, if you don't mind, Skint," Calli said. "Herr Zann, a pleasure to meet you again." She said this like she wasn't facing an obviously decomposing human. "Might I say, it's lovely to see you can speak again."

"Indeed," he said in his sickeningly glottal voice, "though I have suffered some obvious setbacks since my long-ago nights on *Rue d'Auseil,* I have also gained some additional talents." He bent to the larger of the two cases. "Speaking of such, shall we?"

Calli made a bowing motion. Skint simply stood back, watching, waiting for what came out of the case.

Whatever he was expecting, what Zann pulled out was absolutely not what he was expecting.

♦♦♦

SKINT PUT HIS hands up to cover the...thing...that Zann had produced from the case. "Shit, mate, what the hell kind travesty is that thing? Put it away, man! Put it away!"

Zann held the thing up. His delicate hands didn't seem to hold it by its surface, but more to sink into its hide.

"This is your instrument, Herr Flynt," he said, sounding hurt by Skint's rejection. "It is what you will play for the Master."

"Skint," Calli said. "We would have brought your guitar had we been able to. We couldn't, so I had to make do. Herr Zann is saving our butts here, so please. Take the instrument."

Zann held it out with both hands, a hopeful smile creasing his rotting lips.

Skint reached out gingerly, and his fingers touched the instrument. It was unpleasantly warm, and slightly moist. And from somewhere inside, there were rhythmic throbs. Then Zann released it, and he had no choice but to bear its odd weight.

He found it hard to look at the thing, because, depending on how it was twisted and turned, parts of it would bend more than the motion called for, and other parts would simply disappear, though he could still feel them, his hand still holding them.

"It's a guitar, Herr Flynt," Zann said, "but it was built on eleven dimensions. I think you'll find its sound extraordinary."

"How the fook am I supposed to even play—"

"Don't think about it," Calli said. "Just close your eyes and play it."

"Just play it, Herr Flynt."

"Play like you're raising the dead, Skint."

Just fuckin' play it. He closed his eyes. *Find the fingering.* His fingers explored the surface of the thing. *You've played everything from a hurdy gurdy to a fuckin' theremin, Skinty, you can wrestle this fucker to the ground.*

He gave it an experimental strum, heard the tuning, but more importantly, heard the motherfucking *tone* of the thing. *Damn.*

He tried a couple of chords. Adjusted them for the tuning, tried them again.

Fuck me, he thought. *Might just work.*

Then he started playing.

♦♦♦

SKINT SWIRLED AROUND the piece that he and Calli had worked out, but much of it was improvised. He had to take this thing for a test drive before he drove it where he needed to.

The additional two strings messed him up to start with, but then he understood how and when to incorporate them. He found there were certain notes or chords that made the instrument spasm or shiver, that added an additional quality to the sound that he could exploit. And if he twisted it just right, to make it take those strange angles or disappearances, it opened up the sound immensely, as though he went from playing in a small room to the most acoustically perfect concert hall.

He noodled for ten or fifteen minutes, mapping out what worked and what didn't.

Then, with a knowing smirk, he gave Calli a wink.

And he played to raise the dead.

♦♦♦

WISH I COULD have a ciggy, he thought. *Or a blunt.* He liked to take a drag now and then, then tuck the butt under the strings at the head. Not that this thing had a head.

A headless demon, Skint thought. Calli had told him about some Irish demons that were headless. The *dullahan.*

And then he had a name for the thing he was playing. A dullahan.

He wound through the opening melody, starting as a slow, throbbing creep, though the melody would come roaring back as he built and built and built on the urgency.

Then there was an evocative counterpoint behind him. At first, he thought it was the dullahan working its magic. It wasn't. He turned, carefully, aware of the sonic change it could inspire, and looked behind him.

Zann was playing a smaller stringed instrument. A viol.

And he was killing it.

He weaved in and out of Skint's melodies, seeming to know when Skint went high and adding a bass rumble that shouldn't have been possible with an instrument that small, but also knowing when Skint went low, and layering a sweet high tone over it. Always complimenting, never overpowering.

Skint gave Zann a smile. Zann met his eyes, but played with a deadly seriousness.

Fuck, if I'd heard this guy in the Seventies, Higgy would have been able to take that choirmaster job at Winchester Cathedral. Zann would have been in The Lema, rotting or not.

Skint kicked it into the next gear, and Zann followed his changes effortlessly.

He shot a look at Calli, to give her some reassurance that it was going fine, but when he met her eyes, they were troubled.

Then she said

♦♦♦

"IT'S NOT WORKING."

What?

He was playing exactly what they'd worked out. Hell, it was even better than they'd worked out, because Zann was shredding that viol, wringing all the blood right out of it.

She gave him a thin-lipped, grim shake of the head. *It's not working.*

On the way here, she'd explained a little more of what they were trying to do.

"We're trying to rouse Cthulhu," she'd said. "Not wake him up, hell no, but dredge him up a bit from full slumber."

"What's that gonna do?" he'd asked.

"It's gonna hopefully solve our Milo problem," she'd said. "Let me worry about that end. What I need you to do is work your magic to raise a dead, yet dreaming god up from...well the sleep of the dead. Basically, I'm asking you to music him back to a semblance of life."

"Music him."

"Best way to describe it."

It's not working.

He was failing.

Failing was something, unfortunately, Skint had begun to become accustomed to. He'd been in the biggest band in the world. His music was still played constantly, half a decade later. Money still came roaring in from royalties and merchandise.

But it was all past glory. All things he'd accomplished a lifetime ago. Now, his new music came and went without so much as a splash or even a mention in *Rolling Stone*. The two other bands he'd created after The Lema are considered jokes at best, and embarrassing at worst. The only thing anyone wanted him to talk about was a band forty years in its grave, along with his drummer and mate, Boomer Williamson.

Everything since had been a slow slide into mediocrity and obscurity.

He couldn't even deal with a shithead who made music with a fucking computer instead of an instrument, autotuned his own voice, and sold twice as many albums as The Lema ever had. Couldn't make him stop playing that embarrassment of a song.

He saw Calli then, the one bright star in his fast-dwindling universe. His friend. His lover. His muse.

And he remembered the night they met.

While anyone else would have seen what she'd done that night—what *they* had done that night—as terrible, as perverted, as depraved and evil, he'd seen it as something wondrous.

She'd taken something dead and somehow made it alive and whole again.

She'd made something positive out of a negative.

She'd created life where life had escaped.

And she'd done the same with Skint. He who had been lost had somehow been found.

He also realized, as all of this flashed across his mind as his fingers flashed across the fretboard, that this was yet another example of what once was dead was now alive.

Calli had done that.

Calli.

His muse.

And now he was playing the song she had given him to do the same thing. To bring the dead to life, if only briefly.

She's given you a gift that once again you're squandering, Skint.

Because he was playing it simply note-for-note.

I gotta add my magic to hers, he realized.

♦ ♦ ♦

LEANING IN TOWARD Calli, Skint said, "Look at me. Watch me."

She turned to him, faced him, her expression worried but hopefully.

He stared directly into her eyes. He thought of that first night, and all the days and nights since then. Thousands of them.

And he *played.*

He watched her face and let his fingers do their thing. They knew where to go, they knew what to do. He could hear it and also sit off to the side and analyze and correct and adjust and sketch out improvements as he went. Add a run here. Tap out a counterpoint here. Back off and hold a sustain here.

But it needed more than just tweaks.

Skint found his spot, and then angled off into completely uncharted territory. Calli's eyes squinted as she first tried to place the sounds, then widened as she realized he was going off-script.

She shook her head in a panicked *no.* Even Zann seemed to falter, then found his place again, weaving his magic with Skint's.

But Skint only saw Calli. He gave her a small nod, far from the cocky one of earlier. This one said, *it's okay. Trust me.*

She nodded back. Then she smiled.

He gave himself a half-second to think, *I love you, Calli.*

And he played.

IT WAS SO subtle initially that Skint thought it was still one of Zann's bass counterpoints, but he slowly became aware of the atonal rumbling thuds.

Just as they were prevalent enough that he noticed them, Calli approached him and gently laid a hand on his left hand. He stopped playing.

"We need to go," she said.

"I'm sorry," Skint said. "I thought it was working. Isn't it working?"

She smiled then. "Oh yes, babe, it worked. That's why we have to go."

Zann was hurriedly packing his viol back into its case. Skint made to hand back the dullahan, but Zann held up a hand. "You've earned the instrument. I will do my best to ensure it follows you back." With a final nod, he said, "Fare well, Herr Flynt. It was an honor to weave this tapestry with you." Then he took a single step back and disappeared.

"We have to leave now."

Skint clutched the dullahan tighter, and followed Calli's lead.

IT MUST HAVE been a crack of thunder that woke him, because he heard the rumbling echo die off, like an amp with faulty wiring. It was a good sound, and he filed it away for use on a future piece.

Apparently Calli had heard the same sound. Once the final rumbles had faded, he felt her as she rolled on her side to face him. She put a hand on his chest and said, "Good morning. How you feeling?"

He searched himself for a moment. "Actually, Cal, I feel fookin' stellar. Best sleep I've had in years."

"Good," she said. "Me too."

"It all happened then, dinnit?"

"It all happened, Skint."

"Fook me." He reached over for his cigarettes, stuck one at the side of his mouth, squinted while he lit it, and took his first drag of the morning. He let the smoke drift lazily out of his nostrils, then he remembered something, snorted the last of it out, and said, "The dullahan?"

Calli pointed. The bizarre instrument was propped against a chair on the far wall. It still hurt his eyes and his brain to look at it.

"Okay," he said, nodding. "Good. That's good then." He wasn't truly sure it was, but he'd take it for now. "And our friend next door?"

Calli raised her head, propped it on her hand. "I'll answer your question with one of my own. What do you hear?"

Skint sat up in the bed, the silk sheets pooling in his lap. He cocked his head as he tapped the ash off his cigarette into an ashtray. "Diddly," he said finally. "I got nothing."

She nodded.

"What did we do?"

"Let's go look."

"WELL FOOK ME sideways," Skint said, but there was a hushed reverence in his voice.

She couldn't really think of an adequate response, so she just said, "yeah."

They both stood at the end of Skint's property, where his met Milo's.

Where it *used* to meet Milo's.

Now, the ground fell away to water, the ocean waves gently lapping at the new shore.

"What'd we do, Cal?"

"You know how there's times when you sleep really deeply, and then there's times where you're almost awake?

"Yeah," Skint said. "Every fookin' night?"

"Right," Calli said. "Well we basically did the same with the Great Old One. We woke him up enough that he had to drop back down into his deep slumber."

"So the Great Cthulhu farted and rolled over?"

"Nothing so crude," she said, but she was smiling. Skint could get away with saying things no one else could. "Cthulhu dreams."

"Yeah," Skint said, then he spit out, "*Ph'nglui mglw'nafh Cthulhu R'lyeh wgah'nagl fhtagn,*" thoroughly mangling it.

"Right," she said, trying not to wince. "But, like you, when he falls into the dreamstate, he's also subject to something similar to myoclonic jerks."

"Say what now?"

"You know how, when you're falling asleep, you kind of jerk your whole body?"

"Ah, right. Ol' Tentacle Face gets them too?"

"He does." She smiled. "But, being a Great Old One, they're more...cataclysmic."

"And what's that got to do with all this?" Skint waved a hand at the change to the real estate.

"Have you not been listening?" She laughed at him. Actually laughed. He loved the sound. "He's a Great Old One, Skint. He's from beyond the stars. When he moves, planets quake."

"An' when he myocolostomy jerks, he turns my place into a fookin' *island*?"

"It's myoclonic, Skint." She sighed. "And, I figured he'd likely wipe Milo off the map, though I didn't anticipate to this degree."

Yeah, Milo took the damn map with him, wherever he went.

They looked out from their vantage point.

"So, that was really fookin' dangerous, what we did, yeh?"

"Little bit," Calli said.

"'Little bit' she says. Like killin' a fookin' bug with a nuclear fookin' bomb, I say."

"It worked, though, didn't it?"

Skint's home and roughly three acres of land remained mostly untouched, aside from some branches that had fallen from some trees, and some of the sod ripped up from wind. But go beyond his property line, and there was nothing but water for at least a half-mile to the north, east, and south, where he previously had neighbours.

His house was now on an island.

"It did at that, Calli," he said. "It did at that."

News helicopters were already approaching from the mainland.

"Where'd he go?" Skint said. "Milo?"

"Might have been simply bulldozed under an onslaught of in-rushing sea," Calli said, shrugging. "Might be on Uranus."

"He was always on my anus, Cal."

She swatted his shoulder.

"And what about Kensington and Simmons?" He pointed first to the south and then to the east, indicating his other two neighbours.

"I could only protect one property," she said. "It was a struggle to even do that. You've got a fair amount of land, Skint." She looked south and east. "Unfortunately, they were unintended casualties."

"S'okay," he said. "I couldn't stand that fookin' dog of Kensington's. It never stopped fookin' barkin'. And Simmons's eyes were too close together," he said, waving his fingers in front of his face. "Couldn't trust 'im."

Calli let the judgements pass. She was honestly surprised the devastation was as localized as it was. California got off light, as far as she was concerned.

And it was a small price to pay to keep Skint happy.

Skint squinted up at the helicopters, said, "Gonna hafta get me one of those, I guess. Make the tennis court into a helipad."

He never played tennis anyway.

He flipped the bird to the news copters, then turned to head back into the house.

"What are you going to do?" she said.

"Get some water and power back to my new island, get some breakfast, then…" he gave her a grin that made her remember why she stayed with him all these years "...then I've got a whole new piece to record with my new dullahan. Reckon I could get Zann to show up?"

Calli looked around at the island. At the now-distant shoreline of California.

"Not a good idea, Skint."

He shrugged. "Worth the ask."

"This new piece," she said. "What will you call it?"

"Been thinkin' on that. I think *Awaken the Dreamer* fits all right, don't it?"

She nodded. It did indeed.

STORY NOTES

I'M GUESSING IT'S not going to take a lot of investigative digging to figure out where the impetus of this story came from.

Yes, it was the clash of Led Zeppelin's Jimmy Page and Robbie Williams, once a member of Take That. They got into some argument over Robbie building stuff on his property that Jimmy thought was going to cause damage to his own. I'll let you look up the details.

For me though, knowing Jimmy was big into Aleister Crowley, I wanted him to start seeking out a more supernatural solution to his problem. I once worked with a woman named Calliope, and I loved the name, so I shamelessly stole it, but decided to mess with her, taking bits from that ol' Lovecraft fella, as well as borrowing a bit from Michael McDowell's awesome Southern Gothic six-book *Blackwater* series.

I had the opening written for the longest time, but didn't know where to take it. Still not sure I'm absolutely happy with where it ended up, but I've gotta say, I had a complete blast writing an over-the-hill classic rock god going up against a more modern day pop star. And Calli? Hell, Calli just wrote herself. I had nothing to do with her.

The ubiquitous and mysterious "they" always say to write to please yourself, and honestly, I think that's great advice. I *do* write to please myself first.

I've been lucky that I've also managed to please a good majority of my readers as well. But sometimes, like the story you just read, sometimes I just have *fun* actually writing the story as well. Yeah, I'm that guy that laughs at my own jokes.

But seriously, Skint was a character I had a blast with, and one of the characters I can see very clearly in my mind.

Anyway, I hope it scratched at least a bit of an itch for you. It's got a lot of fun stuff in it that I didn't expect to see, including a rotting return of Lovecraft's Erich Zann.

If this story doesn't show you how I pull from so many different influences, I truly don't know what will.

END NOTES

AND SO ENDS the first volume of *UGLY STORIES ABOUT TERRIBLE PEOPLE DOING HORRIBLE THINGS.*

This particular collection is a good representative of how long or short I can go, with both the longest non-novel/novella I've written, *Awaken The Dreamer*, as well as the shortest, *Angel*.

This one tends to be kind of all over the map, subject-wise as well, from cosmic horror to time travel, angels to demons, dogs to werewolves, and children to senior citizens.

You've also got some of my oldest stories, right up to one, *Change of Heart*, that I finished just a day before including it in this collection.

I quite enjoyed going back over my output. Some of these stories I'd completely forgotten about. Some still make me wince a bit, but overall, I found something to love in each one.

I hope you did as well, and I hope to welcome you to more of my nightmares in the next volume.

Thanks for reading.

ABOUT THE AUTHOR

TOBIN ELLIOTT WRITES ugly stories about terrible people doing horrible things. He's been doing this for longer than he'd care to admit.

He's managed to even get a bunch of those ugly stories published, placing eight short stories in various anthologies, and three novellas published through small presses.

Over the span of eight months from late 2022 to mid-2023, Tobin independently published a six-book horror series, the *Cycle of the Aphotic World,* to exceptional reviews.

He's hoping to see the non-fiction book he wrote published by a major publisher soon, and he's also working on some very gothic stuff with co-author Robert Edgar Walton.

Keeping in the writing vein, he taught Creative Writing at two different universities for two decades, was a board member for both the Writers' Community of Simcoe County (WCSC) and the Writers' Community of Durham Region (WCDR), and took part in the annual Muskoka Novel Marathon for five years. He was also one-fifth of ID Press, and helped publish three really cool anthologies that he's quite proud of.

Tobin's been married for 33 years, and counts two wonderful adult children amongst his greatest creations.

♦♦♦

REVIEWS ARE INCREDIBLY important to independently-published authors, and Tobin appreciates every one, good, bad, or anything in between.

Please consider rating and/or reviewing this book wherever you can. Every little bit helps.

You can find out more about Tobin here:

https://linktr.ee/TobinElliott

or by scanning the QR code below.

ALSO FROM TOBIN ELLIOTT

BAD BLOOD

THE FIRST BOOK OF THE APHOTIC CYCLE

Sometimes, the ties that bind can break you.

"*BAD BLOOD* is a root canal without the gas that will make you squirm even as you greedily turn the pages for more."
Philip Fracassi, author of *BOYS IN THE VALLEY* and *GOTHIC*

ALSO FROM TOBIN ELLIOTT

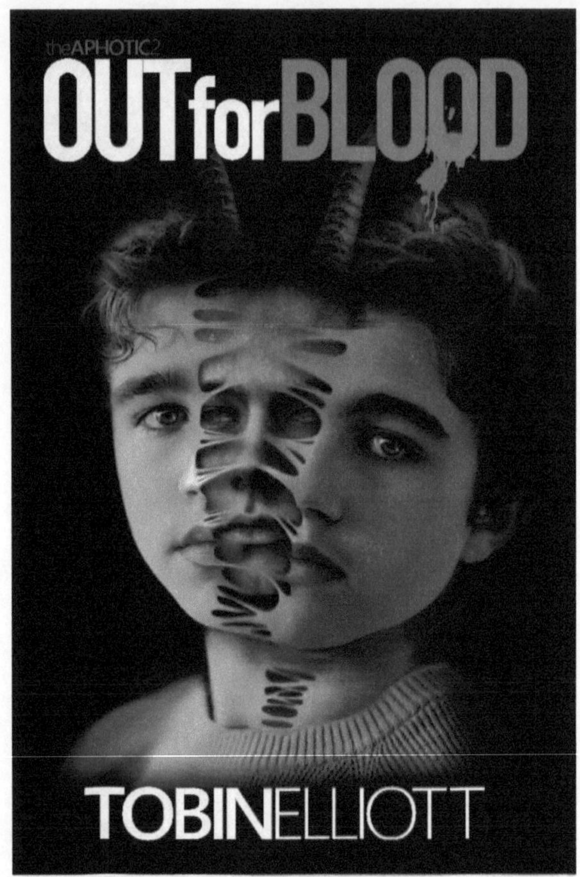

OUT for BLOOD

THE SECOND BOOK OF THE APHOTIC CYCLE

Everyone has their demons. But Stinky Pete released his into the school, and now it's out for blood.

"An exhilarating journey into a world where darkness and mystery collide in a symphony of suspense."
Tamel Wino, author of *ÉKLEIPSIS* and *ÉKLEIPSIS: THE ABYSS*

ALSO FROM TOBIN ELLIOTT

BLOOD LOSS

THE THIRD BOOK OF THE APHOTIC CYCLE

You think you know what it means to lose blood?
Losing blood doesn't always mean you're bleeding.

"Every book in *The Aphotic* series has had a character that I'll never forget. Characters I truly felt for, characters I will remember and look back on as old friends."
Jonny Ward, host of *The Nerdyverse of Madness* podcast

ALSO FROM TOBIN ELLIOTT

BLOOD PACT

THE FOURTH BOOK OF THE APHOTIC CYCLE

Two ancient relics, two feral, supernatural species, one fight for control. Some families are born in blood.

"Tobin Elliott is a gifted storyteller who takes familiar tropes, turns them on their heads, and makes them his own
Danielle Vinson, editor and book reviewer

ALSO FROM TOBIN ELLIOTT

BLOOD RELATIONS

THE FIFTH BOOK OF THE APHOTIC CYCLE

Whoever said you can't go home again was right. Lex tried. And now she really wishes she hadn't.

"When I thought it couldn't get any better here comes Tobin and [the fifth book] of *The Aphotic* series. Wow!!! I have to give it to Tobin, the man can definitely write."
Damaris Quinones, book reviewer

ALSO FROM TOBIN ELLIOTT

FLESH and BLOOD

THE SIXTH AND FINAL BOOK OF THE APHOTIC CYCLE

Sometimes, talking to the right person can show you a path out of darkness...but what if that person has been dead for thirty years?

"Tobin Elliott explores the fascinating juxtaposition between the family we're born with and the family we choose, all the while delivering on everything he promised in the previous five books. *FLESH AND BLOOD* is a perfect conclusion to one of the greatest horror series I've ever read."
David Buzan, author of *IN THE LAIR OF LEGENDS*

ALSO FROM TOBIN ELLIOTT

UGLY STORIES ABOUT TERRIBLE PEOPLE DOING HORRIBLE THINGS VOLUME TWO

"[*Ugly Stories Vol 2*] is an anxiety-spiked, claustrophobic, emotionally damaging experience. Got any traumatic scars? Elliott's got a scalpel poised to pick 'em apart."
Diane Klaver, ARC reader

www.ingramcontent.com/pod-product-compliance
Lightning Source LLC
Chambersburg PA
CBHW030132010826
48973CB00002B/532

* 9 7 8 1 9 9 8 8 2 7 0 8 4 *